THE LOTTERY TICKET

Which he drank to the last drop.

Frontispiece.

THE LOTTERY TICKET

JULES VERNE

WILDSIDE PRESS

Published by
Wildside Press
P.O. Box 301
Holicong, PA 18928-0301 U.S.A.
www.wildsidepress.com

MEET JULES VERNE

Jules Verne (1828-1905) was a French writer and one of the founding fathers of science fiction, although, surprisingly, his only novel about the future, *Paris in the 21st Century* (1863) was rejected in his lifetime and not actually published until 1994. He was trained in law and briefly worked as a stockbroker, but soon committed himself to literature. After a brief start with short stories and plays he came to specialize in "Voyages Extraordinaires," which combined adventure and travel writing with his enthusiasm for scientific discovery and new technology. His best-known works include *A Journey to the Center of the Earth* (1864), *From the Earth to the* Moon (1865), Twenty *Thousand Leagues under the Sea* (1870), *Around the World in Eighty Days* (1872), and *The Mysterious Island* (1875). All of these have been filmed repeatedly, with great success.

Not all of Verne's novels, or even all the "Voyages" contain fantastic elements. Indeed, one of his most popular novels has always been *Michael Strogoff* (1876) is an adventure story, set in Russia, and there is nothing quite fantastic in *Around the World in Eighty Days*, although the conclusion hinges on a scientific point, that the hero gained a day by crossing the International Date Line in an easterly direction. It also inspired a science fictional sequel, *The Other Log of Phineas Fogg* by Philip Jose Farmer (1973). Verne transported his readers to places they had never been, into situations few had imagined, although his stories were set in his own time, in hidden corners of the world. What makes him more than an adventure writer, of course, is the speculative elements: Captain Nemo's submarine, lunar flight, the massive flying machine (an aerial battleship) in *Robur the Conqueror* (1886) and *Master of the World* (1904). The lesser-known *The Begum's Fortune* (1879) involves an attempt to create two "utopian" communities (in the Cascades, in Oregon, which seemed remote enough to French readers of Verne's time), one of them run by a mad German militarist who develops super-weapons. If you consider the repeating motif here, of a super-scientist outcast/misanthrope with an exotic, secret base, a small army of devoted followers, and super-scientific weapons or other technology far in advance of the rest of the world, one might consider that, for all Captain Nemo is somewhat sympathetic and Robur proposes to subdue the world to put an end to war, Verne came very close to inventing the James Bond villain. All he needed was a secret-agent hero to bring such reigns of terror to an end.

Verne's work was enormously influential. M.P. Shiel's *The Lord of the Sea* (1901), for example, would not possibly have existed without the example of Verne's Robur and Nemo. The novels of George Griffith, *The Angel of the Revolution* (1893) and any of a number of other late Victorian stories about aerial warfare owe much to *Robur the Conqueror.* Verne was the predecessor of modern "hard" science fiction, since he insisted that what happened in his stories be scientifically plausible. He was reported to have sneered at the anti-gravity metal, "cavorite," used to propel a spaceship in H.G. Wells' *The First Men in the Moon* (1901), "Let him produce it." Wells might have asked how Captain Nemo's *Nautilus* is powered. Like most hard-sf writers, Verne was capable of stretching things a bit when a good story required it, and he was, above all else, a superb storyteller.

His reputation has always been high in France and in much of the rest of Europe, if ill-served in the English-speaking world by bad 19th century translations, and the tendency to relegate his books to the Boys Adventure category, which tends to overlook the richness of his ideas and his frequently caustic satire. He has been the subject of renewed critical attention in recent years, and remains a seminal figure.

—Darrell Schweitzer

THE LOTTERY TICKET.

CHAPTER I.

"WHAT time is it?" asked Dame Hansen, as she knocked the ashes out of her pipe while the last few whiffs floated off against the painted beams of the ceiling.

"Eight o'clock, mother," answered Hulda.

"No travellers will come to-night; the weather is so bad."

"So I think. If they do, the rooms are ready, and I shall be sure to hear if any one calls."

"Has your brother come back?"

"Not yet."

"Did he say he would to-day?"

"No, mother; Joel has gone with a tourist to Lake Tinn, and as he started late I do not see how he could get home before to-morrow."

"Is he going to sleep at Mœl?"

"Perhaps; unless he goes to Bamble and calls on Farmer Helmboë—"

"And on his daughter—"

"Yes, on Siegfrid, my best of friends, whom I love as if she were my sister!" answered the girl as she smiled.

"Well, shut the door, Hulda, and let us go to bed."

"Are you ill, mother?"

"No, but in the morning I want to be up early. I must go to Mœl—"

"What for?"

"Eh? Haven't I got to buy the things for the season now beginning?"

"Has the Christiania carrier arrived at Mœl with the wine and provisions?"

"Yes, this afternoon," said Dame Hansen. "Leng-ling, the overseer at the saw-mill, told me so as he passed. We are nearly out of hams and smoked salmon, and I don't want to be found without anything in the house. When the weather mends tourists will soon begin coming into Tellemarken, and our house must be fit to receive them, and we must have everything they are likely to want. You know very well it is the 15th of April."

"The 15th of April!" sighed the girl.

"So to-morrow I shall have to see about these things," continued Dame Hansen; "it will only take me a couple of hours to make my purchases, and the carrier can bring them while I return with Joel in the carriole."

"If you meet the postman, mother, don't forget to ask him if he has a letter for us—"

"Or for you rather! And that is not unlikely, for Ole's last letter was a month ago."

"Yes, a month! a whole month!"

"Don't worry yourself, Hulda. The delay is not very wonderful. Besides, if the Mœl postman has nothing for us, what doesn't come by Christiania may come by Bergen."

"Perhaps, mother ; but what would you have me do ?
My heart is heavy because Newfoundland is so far
away. A whole ocean to cross, and the weather still
bad ! It is nearly a year since my poor Ole went, and
who can tell when he will come back to us at Dal—"

"And whether we shall be here when he does come
back?" murmured Dame Hansen, but so gently that
her daughter could not hear her.

Hulda rose and shut the door which opened on to the
Vestfjorddal road. She did not take the trouble to turn
the key. In hospitable Norway such precautions are
unnecessary. By day or night the traveller can enter
where he will, and there is no waiting for the door to be
unlocked. No fear of thieves exists even in the remotest
districts, and no unlawful attempt against either goods
or person ever troubles the security of the people.

Mother and daughter occupied two rooms on the first
floor in the front of the inn, not elaborately furnished,
but testifying unmistakably to a good housewife's care.
Joel's room was overhead just under the roof, which
projected like that of a chalet. It was lighted by a
single window set in a carved frame, and from it the
splendid view ranged from the distant mountain horizon
down into the neighbouring narrow valley through which
roared the torrential Maan. A clumsy flight of wooden
stairs, with steps polished till they shone again, led from
the ground to the rooms above.

Dame Hansen, taking up a coloured glass candlestick
had begun to ascend the stairs, when she was stopped
midway by a knock at the door, and a shout without
of,—

"Dame Hansen ! Dame Hansen !"

"Who comes so late?" said she, turning to go down.

"Has anything happened to Joel?" asked Hulda, as she ran to the door.

There she saw a young lad whom she recognized as a skydskarl, that is to say, one of those boys who hang on behind the carrioles and bring back the horses when the stage is finished. He had arrived on foot and was standing at the threshold.

"What do you want at this time of night?" asked Hulda.

"To wish you good evening."

"Is that all?"

"No! that is not all, but isn't it always proper to be civil to begin with?"

"Oh, yes! But who sent you?"

"Your brother Joel."

"Joel? and why?" asked Dame Hansen.

She came to the door with that slow, measured step peculiar to the Norwegians. The reply had evidently startled her, and she continued quickly,—

"Has anything happened to my son?"

"Yes. He has had a letter brought by the Christiania carrier from Drammen—"

"A letter from Drammen?" said she, lowering her voice.

"I don't know," said the lad; "all I know is that Joel will not be back till to-morrow, and that he sent me here with the letter."

"It is urgent, then?"

"Seems so."

"Give it to me," said the dame, in a tone of great uneasiness.

" There it is, clean and uncrumpled. Only it is not for you."

Dame Hansen seemed to breathe more easily.

" And who is it for ? "

" Your daughter."

" For me ! " said Hulda. " It's a letter from Ole I'm sure, a letter come through Christiania! My brother wouldn't keep me waiting for it."

Hulda took the letter, and after holding it up to the light on the table, looked at the address.

" Yes. It is from him ! Really from him ! Perhaps it tells us when the *Viking* is coming back ! "

As she looked at the letter, Dame Hansen said to the boy, " Will you not come in ? "

" Only for a minute. I must get back home to-night, for I am engaged for a carriole in the morning."

" Well, then, tell Joel that I intend to meet him; and that he is to wait for me."

" To-morrow night ? "

" No, to-morrow morning. He is not to leave Mœl till he has seen me, and we will come back to Dal together."

" All right."

" Have a nip of brandy ? "

" Yes, please."

The lad approached the table, and Dame Hansen poured him out a little of the spirit, which he drank to the last drop.

" *God aften !* " he said.

" *God aften*, my boy ! "

And with this, the Norwegian good-night, given without even a bow or a nod, or a sign of recognition, the youngster left, and soon his footsteps were lost beneath the trees which shaded the footpath by the torrent side.

Meanwhile Hulda gazed at Ole's letter and made no haste to open it. Of what was she thinking? The frail envelope had crossed an ocean to reach her. She looked at the different postmarks. Posted on the 15th of March, it had arrived at Dal on the 15th of April. A month had gone since Ole had written. What might have happened during that month on the coasts of Newfoundland! It was there still winter and the equi-noctial gales were to come; the fishing grounds are the most dangerous places in the world owing to the terrific gales that sweep on to them from across the North American plains. A hard, dangerous life is that of a fisherman, and if Ole followed it, was it not to bring his earnings to her, his betrothed, to marry her when he returned? Poor Ole! what did he say in his letter? Most likely that he loved Hulda as Hulda loved him, that their thoughts were ever of each other despite the distance between them, and that he wished it were the day of his arrival at Dal!

Yes! He would say all that. Hulda was sure. But perhaps he would add that his return was near at hand, that the fishing season which takes the men of Bergen so far from their native land would soon be over. Perhaps Ole would say that the *Viking* had fully stowed her cargo and was preparing to start, and that before the end of April they would be in each other's arms in this happy home in Vestfjorddal? Perhaps he would say that she could fix the day when the pastor could come from Mœl and unite them in the little wooden chapel, the tower of which rose from the thick clump of trees a few hundred yards from Dame Hansen's inn ?

To know all this she had only to open the envelope, and, through her tears either of grief or joy as the case might be, to read the letter. And assuredly more than one impatient girl of the South, of Dalecarlia, of Denmark, or of Holland would already have known what the young Norwegian still knew not ! but Hulda was in a dream, and dreams only end when it pleases Heaven.

"Well, daughter," said the Dame, "is that a letter from Ole ? "

" Yes. I know his handwriting."

" And are you going to wait till to-morrow to read it ? "

Hulda gave the envelope a last look, and then very leisurely tore it open and drew forth a carefully written letter, which she read as follows :—

"Saint Pierre Miquelon, 17th March, 1862.

"DEAREST HULDA,—You will be delighted to know that our fishing has prospered, and that in a day or two we shall have finished. It is nearly all over. After a year away how glad I shall be to get back to Dal, to the only family which remains to me—and which is thine. My share of the profits turns out well, and will do to start us in housekeeping. Messrs. Help Brothers, our owners at Bergen, have been advised that the *Viking* will be home from the 15th to the 20th of May. You can expect to see me about then, that is to say in a few weeks from this.

" Dearest Hulda, I hope to find you looking even better than when I left you, and that like your mother you will be in good health. And I hope to find in good health my cousin Joel, your brother. who wishes for nothing better than to be my brother. Please give my kind regards to Dame Hansen, who I can see now in her arm-chair near the old stove in the big room. Tell her that I love her twice over, first, for being your mother, secondly, for being my aunt. Do not come to Bergen to meet me. It may be that the *Viking* may get home before the date I have given. Whatever may happen, I shall be with you at Dal within twenty-four hours of my landing.

" We have had a rough time of it from the storms, which have been the worst our men remember. Fortunately, the cod on the Grand Bank has been abundant. The *Viking* brings home five thousand quintals to Bergen, which have already been all sold by Help Brothers, and what will interest you most, the profit has been large. If I am not bringing a fortune home, I have an idea, or rather a presentiment, that one is waiting for me when I return. Yes! a fortune, to say nothing of happiness! What do you mean ? you say. Well, that is my secret, dearest, and you will forgive me for having a secret from you. It is the only one! Besides, I will tell you —when ?—when the time comes—before our marriage if it is delayed—after it, if I get back at the time stated, and if in the week following my return to Dal you become my wife, as I so hope you will.

" Would my arms were round you, Hulda ! Embrace for me your mother and my cousin Joel. I send you a kiss for your forehead, on which the radiant crown of the brides of Tellemarken will look like the halo of a saint. For the last time, dearest Hulda, good-bye !

"Your betrothed,

"OLE KAMP."

CHAPTER II.

DAL has but few houses,—some of them straggling along
the road, which is little more than a footpath, some
dotted here and there on the neighbouring ridges, all of
them facing the narrow valley of Vestfjorddal, while
behind them range away the northern hills with the river
flowing at their feet. The little wooden church, built
in 1855, has a chancel lighted by two narrow windows,
and is crowned with a square steeple, which stands boldly
up amid the trees. The brooks as they rush down to
join the river are crossed by tiny wooden bridges, trellised
in lozenge fashion, with the intersections filled in with
moss-grown stones. From the distance is heard the
hum of several rough sawmills, worked by the mountain
torrents, with one wheel to drive the saw and another to
drive the timber as it is being cut. Church, sawmills,
houses, and sheds all seem bathed in a vaporous sea of
verdure, purplish with the pines and greyish-green with
the birches, which singly and in clumps extend from
the winding banks of the Maan up to the crests of the
high mountains of Tellemarken. Such is the hamlet of
Dal with its picturesque dwellings ; gaily painted all of
them, some in delicate hues, light green and faint rose,
others in gorgeous colouring of vivid yellow or blood
red ; with roofs of birch bark covered with green turf, and
gay with wild flowers rising amid the grass which
yields its autumn crop to the scythe. It is a beautiful

spot in the most charming country in the world. For
Dal is in Tellemarken, Tellemarken is in Norway, and
Norway is another Switzerland, with thousands of fjords,
which bring in the sea to the very feet of its mountains.

Tellemarken is in that bold curve of the coast which
Norway makes between Bergen and Christiania. It has
mountains and glaciers like Switzerland, only it is not
Switzerland. It has waterfalls as grand as those of
America, but it is not America. It has landscapes with
painted houses and people with costumes of the past
like many a town in Holland, but it is not Holland.
Tellemarken is better than all these. It is Tellemarken,
itself a country alone in this world for the natural
beauties with which it is gifted. The author has had
the pleasure of visiting it. He has posted through it in
a carriole ; and he brought away with him an impression
of poetry and charm that he would willingly throw into
this simple narrative.

At the time of the story, 1862, Norway had not been
traversed by the railway, which now runs from Stockholm to Drontheim by way of Christiania. Now a huge
chain of rails is stretched across the two Scandinavian
countries which are little inclined to live their lives
together. But, though the tourist may travel faster shut
up in the railway carriage than if he were in a carriole,
he sees nothing of the old ways of communication. He
loses the southern journey across Sweden by the curious
Gotha canal, dragged by the steamboat from lock to
lock to a height of three hundred feet ; and he stops
neither at the falls of Trolletann, at Drammen, nor
Kongsberg, nor at any of the marvels of Tellemarken.

In 1862 the railway was merely a project. Some twenty years were to elapse before it was to be possible to cross the Scandinavian kingdoms from shore to shore in forty hours, and to see the North Cape by return ticket; Dal was then—and may it be so for many years —the central point of attraction for tourists, either foreigners or natives, the latter being chiefly students at Christiania. Thence they could strike off over the whole of Tellemarken and Hardanger, explore the valley of Vestfjorddal between Lake Mjös and Lake Tinn, and visit the wonderful waterfalls of the Rjukan. In the hamlet there was but one inn, but it was as inviting and comfortable as could be desired, and boasted four beds for the accommodation of travellers. In short, the inn was Dame Hansen's.

A few benches stood around the base of the rough woodwork which was cut off from the ground by a solid granite foundation. The pine beams and planks which formed its walls had with time acquired a hardness which defied even the axe. Between the beams, which had been merely squared and laid horizontally one on the other, there was a rejointing of mosses and clay stopping, that would keep out the roughest of the winter rains. Above the windows the zigzag plaster was painted red and black, contrasting with the lighter gayer colours of the paneling. In one corner of the large room the circular stove sent forth its pipe to join on to the kitchen flue; in another the large box-clock stroked its patterned hands round its enamelled face, and marked the seconds with a loud tick-tack. An old writing-desk with brown mouldings stood near the massive painted iron. On a shelf stood a candlestick in terra-cotta, which

B

could be turned into a three-branched one if required. The best furniture in the house was in this room ; the table of birch root with the bent legs, the old chest with ornamental clasps in which were stowed away the best dresses for Sundays and holidays ; the large arm-chair hard as a church seat, the painted wooden chairs, the rustic spinning wheel, ornamented in green so as to stand boldly out against the spinner's red petticoat. Here the pot for the butter and there the rolling pin to squeeze it, here the tobacco box, and the grater of carved bone. Just above the door leading to the kitchen was a large dresser laid out with rows of bright tin and copper utensils, dishes and plates in enamel, crockery and wood, the little grindstone for sharpening, half-hidden in its varnished snail, and the solemn old egg-cup which might do duty for a chalice. And what strange walls covered with linen tapestry, representing subjects from the Bible in all the colours of the rainbow ! The rooms for the travellers, though much simpler, were just as comfortable with their scanty furniture so engagingly clean, their curtains of green verdure hanging from the grass plots on the roof, their large white-sheeted beds, and their panels with verses of the Old Testament written in yellow on a red ground. It should not be forgotten that the floors of the rooms were strewn with small branches of birch, fir, and juniper, and the house was filled with the invigorating fragrance of their leaves.

Could one imagine a more charming posada in Italy or a more attractive fonda in Spain ? No ! and the flood of English tourists had not then arrived to raise the prices, as they had done in Switzerland. At Dal it was not the pound sterling that the traveller's purse was soon bereaved of, but that species of the genus which is worth about five shillings, and whose subdivisions are the mark worth about a franc, and the copper skilling, which is not to be confounded with the British shilling, for it is only worth a halfpenny. Nothing was then to be seen of the pretentious bank-note, of which the tourist in Tellemarken was to make use and—abuse; then only were visible the notes of which one kind is white, one blue, one yellow, one green, and one red; two more, and they would be of all the colours of the rainbow!

And then—and it was a point not to be despised—the food at this hospitable house was better than in most inns of the district. In fact Tellemarken only too well justifies its nickname of the "Land of Clotted Cream." In the valley of the Tiness, the Listhüs, the Tinoset, and many others there is no bread, or it is so bad that it is uneatable. Nothing but oatcake, the "flat bread," dry, black, hard as a board, or even a commoner cake made of the inner bark of the birch mixed with lichens and choppings of straw; rarely eggs, except such as have been laid a week before; but in abundance, inferior beer, clotted cream, sweet or sour, and occasionally a little coffee, so thick that it might be described as a soot distilled from the products of Mocha, Bourbon, or the Rio Nunez.

At Dame Hansen's, however, the cellar and the larder were properly furnished. What could visitors require more? There was cooked salmon, salted or smoked, hores, salmon from the lakes which had never known sea-water, fish from the streams of Tellemarken, fowls neither too tough nor too skinny, eggs in a dozen ways, cakes of rye and cakes of barley-meal, fruits and more especially strawberries, brown bread of excellent quality, beer, and bottles of that old wine of St. Julien which keeps alive the reputation of the French brands, even in these distant countries.

And so the reputation of the inn at Dal had spread in all the countries of northern Europe, as could be seen by turning over the yellow leaves of the visitors' book, wherein the travellers willingly put their names to any compliment paid to Dame Hansen. Generally these were Swedes and Norwegians from all parts of Scandinavia. English there were in great numbers, and one of them, having had to wait an hour on the summit of Gousta for the morning mists to vanish, had written on one of the pages, "Patientia omnia vincit;" and a few Frenchmen there were, one of whom, who had best be anonymous, had written, "Nous n'avons qu'à nous louer de la réception qu'on nous a 'fait' dans cette auberge." The grammatical error matters little after all. If the phrase is more grateful than French, it renders none the less homage to Dame Hansen and her daughter, the charming Hulda of Vestfjorddal.

CHAPTER III.

WITHOUT going too deeply into ethnology, it is easy to believe with many scientists that some relationship exists between the chief families of the English aristocracy and the old families of Scandinavia. Numerous proofs of this exist in the names of ancestors, which in both countries are identical. But there is no aristocracy in Norway. All are equal from the highest to the lowest. In the humblest hut there still hangs the genealogical tree which has in no way degenerated for having been transplanted into plebeian soil. There, in all their quarterings, are the arms of the noble families of feudal times from which the present peasants are descended.

Thus it was with the Hansens of Dal, related in a very distant degree to those English peers whose ancestors came over with the Conqueror. If they no longer possessed neither the position nor the wealth, they still retained the original pride or rather the dignity which is never out of place in life.

Little did it matter, however. Whatever might have been the high birth of his ancestors, Harald Hansen was none the less a simple innkeeper of Dal. The house had come down to him from his father and his grand-father, whose position in the country he remembered with no shame. After him his wife had continued the business in a way to retain the public esteem.

Had Harald made his fortune at the trade? No one knew. But he had been able to bring up his son Joel and his daughter Hulda without their early life being a hard one; and his wife's sister's son, Ole Kamp, had been adopted by him from his earliest years and brought up with his own children. Had it not been for his Uncle Harald, the orphan would have probably been one of those poor little creatures who only come into the world to leave it in early youth. For his adopted parents Ole Kamp was quite filially grateful, nothing could ever break the tie which united him to the Hansens; and his marriage with Hulda would draw it even closer and knot it for life.

Harald had been dead about eighteen months. Besides the inn at Dal he had left his widow a small sœter up in the hills. A sœter is an isolated farm, generally of poor reputation, if it is of any reputation at all. The recent seasons had not been good. All the crops had suffered, even the grass crop. They had had many of those "nights of iron," as the Norwegian peasant calls them, nights of bitter wind and ice, killing off every germ save those deepest in the ground, and bringing ruin to the peasants of Tellemarken and Hardanger.

Although Dame Hansen knew how she was placed she said nothing to anybody about it, not even to her own children. Of a cold, taciturn disposition, she was not very communicative—as Hulda and Joel knew to their sorrow. But with that respect for the head of the family innate among the people of the north, they had maintained a reserve on the subject, though to them it was painful to do so. The dame never asked any one willingly for advice, being absolutely convinced of the safety of her own judgment—in the true Norwegian style.

The dame was then in her fiftieth year. Age had not bowed her tall stature if it had whitened her hair, nor had it subdued the vivacity of the glance from her deep blue eyes, whose azure reappeared unchanged in the eyes of her daughter. Her complexion had, however, taken that clouded yellowish tint which we see in some old law papers, and just a few wrinkles had appeared on her forehead.

The dame, as she was invariably called in Scandinavian fashion, invariably wore a much pleated black petticoat in sign of the mourning which she had never left off since Harald's death. Sleeves of unbleached cotton issued from her brown bodice, a neckerchief of dark colour was crossed on her breast, and this was covered by the bib of an apron fastened behind by large hooks. She always wore a bonnet of thick silk, a sort of cowl, which is gradually falling into disuse. Upright in her wooden chair the grave hostess of Dal only left her spinning-wheel to smoke a little pipe of birch bark and sit amid the light cloud she blew. In truth the house would have been dull enough without the presence of the two children.

Five-and-twenty years old, well set, tall like all the Norwegian mountaineers, bold without swagger, and fearless without being rash, a fine fellow was Joel Hansen with his almost chestnut hair, and his deep dark-blue eyes. His clothes showed off to perfection his powerful shoulders and capacious chest, and the limbs trained to perfection by laborious ascents of the

mountains of Tellemarken. In his ordinary costume
he might have been taken for a trooper, with his tight-
fitting bluish jacket and shoulder-straps, the jacket
crossed on the chest by two long vertical flaps, and
trimmed behind with a design in colours, like some of
the Celtic waistcoats of Brittany. His yellow breeches
were fastened below the knee with a garter and buckle.
His hat was wide-brimmed with black cord and red
edging; and his dress was completed by the fustian
gaiters and strong soled boots, with iron tips, and instep
almost indistinguishable under the folding of the leather.

Joel by trade was a guide in the district of Tellemarken. Ever ready to start, ever indefatigable, he
might have been compared to that Norse hero, Rolf the
Ganger, so famous in the legends of the country. At
times he accompanied such English sportsmen as came
hither to shoot the "riper" or ptarmigan, bigger than
those in the Hebrides, or the "jerper" or partridge, more
delicate than the Scotch grouse. In winter time he was
out wolf-hunting, when the wolves driven by hunger
ventured on the surface of the frozen lakes. In summer
he was out after the bears, when the old animals and
their little ones came down in search of the fresh herbage.
He had often chased them across the lofty plateaux,
and more than once he had owed his life to his prodigious strength which had enabled him to withstand
the embrace of these formidable beasts, and to his
imperturbable coolness which had enabled him to
escape from danger. When there was no tourist to
guide through the valley of Vestfjorddal, and no sports-
man to accompany into the fields, Joel was at work on
the little sœter up the mountains a few miles away.

He owed his life to his prodigious strength.

Page 24.

There a young shepherd employed by Dame Hansen
was engaged in herding half-a-dozen cows and some
thirty sheep, the sœter consisting only of a patch of
pasturage.

Joel was known in all the gaards of Tellemarken, and
as he was of a singularly kind and obliging disposition,
he was well liked everywhere. There were two people
in the world for whom his affection was boundless.
These were his cousin Ole and his sister Hulda. When
Ole Kamp had last left Dal it was greatly to Joel's
regret that he could not give Hulda a marriage portion,
so as to keep her betrothed at home. In fact if he had
been trained to the sea he would not have hesitated to
take his cousin's place. But money was needed to start
the new house and Ole had to cross the Atlantic ; Joel
had gone with him to the end of the valley on the road
to Bergen. There after a long embrace he had wished
him a pleasant voyage and a happy home-coming ; and
then he had returned to console his sister whom he loved
with quite brotherly and fatherly affection.

Hulda was then eighteen. She was not the "piga,"
as they call the servant in the Norwegian inns, but
rather the "fröken," the English "miss," as her mother
was the "madame" of the house. A charming face was
hers, framed with its blonde hair just tinged with gold,
which fell from the light linen cap untied behind so as
to let the plaits hang down ; a lovely form was hers with
the bodice of red stuff and green edging, cut to the
figure, open in front, trimmed with coloured embroidery,
and surmounted by a white chemisette, with the sleeves
clasped to the wrists by a bracelet of ribbons. Round
her waist was the red belt with silver filagree clasps,

which held up the greenish petticoat doubled by an
apron of multi-coloured diamonds ; beneath showed the
white stockings and the slender pointed shoes peculiar
to Tellemarken.

Her maidenly reserve in no way detracted from the
grace with which she received the guests of a day at the
hostelry of Dal. She was well known in the tourist
world, and it had become quite an attraction to shake
hands with the Hulda, the blonde ; and afterwards to
say to her,—

"Thank you for this meal. *Tack for mad !*"

And nothing was more pleasing than to hear her
answer with her fresh sonorous voice,—

"May it do you good. *Wed bekomme !*"

CHAPTER IV.

OLE KAMP had been away for a year. As he had said in his letter, a terrible ordeal is this winter campaign off the shores of Newfoundland. When the money is earnt there, it is earnt well. The gales sweep down on the vessels so suddenly that a whole fishing fleet may be destroyed in a few hours. But the fish swarm on the banks, and when the crews are in luck there is a plenteous reward for all their toils and privations.

And the Norwegians are good seamen. They never fail you when they are wanted. Among the fjords of the coast from Christiania to the North Cape, among the reefs of Finmark and the channels of the Loffoden, there is no want of opportunity for becoming acquainted with the perils of the sea. When they cross the North Atlantic to the distant fisheries of Newfoundland, they have already proved their courage. During their childhood they have been so storm-tossed on the European coast that they are well able to face the tempest on the American fishing-grounds.

And the Norwegians have something to boast of besides. Their ancestors were gallant seamen when the Hanse towns had monopolized the commerce of northern Europe. They may have been little better than pirates in those days, but then piracy was the usual way of business. Since then, commerce has become so demoralized, that we may well imagine something more

remains to be done. Anyhow, the Norwegians were
bold navigators, they are so to-day, and they always
will be so. Ole Kamp was not the man to belie the
promises of his birth. His apprenticeship, his initiation
to this hard life he owed to his father, a captain in the
coasting-trade at Bergen. His infancy had been passed
at this port, which is one of the most frequented in
Scandinavia. Before he took to the sea he had been a
daring youngster on the fjords, a robber of the nests of
aquatic birds, a catcher of the innumerable fish which
are used for stock-fish. As soon as he was old enough
to become a cabin-boy he had sailed on the Baltic, and
the North Sea, even into the Polar Ocean. His father
died. His mother was no more. The young orphan
was then adopted by Harald Hansen ; but, by arrange-
ment with his uncle, he did not give up his trade of the
sea.

When he was ashore he never failed to come back to
Dal to the family he loved, the only one that remained
to him in the world. He made many voyages in the
large fishing boats, and obtained the grade of master
when he was one-and-twenty. He was now twenty-three.

And when he was at Dal what a companion he was
for Joel ! He accompanied him in his journeys across
the mountains up to the highest summits of Tellemarken.
Field and fjord all came alike to the young sailor, and
he never remained behind unless it was to be with his
cousin Hulda.

A close friendship sprang up between Ole and Joel,
and in consequence the sentiment took another form
with the sister. And Joel did his best to encourage it.
Could the girl have found in the whole province a

better lad, a more sympathetic nature, a more devoted character or a warmer heart? If Ole were her husband, Hulda's happiness was assured. And so mother and son agreed to let her inclinations go unchecked.

The people of the North may be undemonstrative, but it is not just to accuse them of insensibility. It is only their way, and it may be as good a way as any other.

It happened, then, that one day the four were seated in the large room, when Ole said, without any preliminary,—

"I have an idea, Hulda."

"What is it?" asked the girl.

"I think you and I ought to get married."

"So do I."

"Agreed," added Dame Hansen, as if the matter had been fully discussed beforehand.

"In that way, Ole," said Joel, "I shall naturally become your brother-in-law."

"Yes," said Ole, "and it is not improbable, Joel, that I shall like you all the better for it."

"If that is possible!"

"Well, you will see."

"I ask nothing better!" answered Joel, shaking hands with Ole.

"Then it is understood, Hulda?" asked Dame Hansen.

"Yes, mother," answered the girl.

"You think so, Hulda!" continued Ole, "I have loved you for such a long time without telling you so."

"And so have I."

"How it came about I don't know."

"Neither do I."

"Perhaps, Hulda, it was because I saw you grow prettier and prettier every year, and better and better."

"You are going crazy, my dear Ole !"

"No, and I can tell you so without making you blush, for it is true. Didn't you see, Dame Hansen that I loved Hulda ? "

"A little."

"And you, Joel ? "

"I ? Very much ! "

"Then," frankly said she with a smile, "you should have warned me."

"But your spells at sea ! " said Dame Hansen, "will they not be hateful to you when you are married ? "

"So much so," answered Ole, "that after the marriage I go abroad no more."

"You will not go abroad again ? "

"No, Hulda ; will it not be impossible for me to leave you alone for so many months ? "

"Then this is the last time you are going to sea ? "

"Yes, but with more of a chance, for this time I may do some good for myself as Messrs. Help Brothers have promised me a share in all due form—"

"They are good people," said Joel.

"None better," answered Ole, "and well known and appreciated by every sailor in Bergen."

"And then, dear Ole," said Hulda, "when you don't go to sea, what are you going to do ? "

"Become Joel's companion. I have good legs, and if they are not good enough, I will go into training. I have an idea that may not turn out so badly : why should we not set up a service of messengers between Drammen,

Kongsberg, and the gaards of Tellemarken! Commu·
nication now is neither easy nor regular, and we might
make something out it. Besides, I have other ideas
without saying anything of—"

"Of what ? "

"Nothing! You will see when I get back. But I
should like you to know that I have made up my mind
for Hulda to be the most envied woman in the country.
Yes ! I have made up my mind about that."

"That will be easy," answered Hulda, giving him her
hand. "Is it not already half done, and is there a
happier house than our house at Dal ? "

Dame Hansen for a moment looked away.

"And so," continued Ole, "it is all arranged?"

"Yes," said Joel.

"And we have nothing else to say ! "

"Nothing."

"You are not sorry, Hulda ? "

"Not at all."

"As to fixing the day, I think we had better wait till
you come ashore again," added Joel.

"Be it so, but something serious will have happened
if, before a year is over, I have not taken Hulda to the
church at Mœl, where our friend Father Andresen will
not refuse to say his best prayers for us."

And that is how they arranged the marriage of Hulda
Hansen and Ole Kamp.

Eight days afterwards the young sailor had to rejoin
his ship at Bremen. But before he left the young
couple had been betrothed with the usual Scandinavian
ceremonies.

In simple, honest Norway, it is the custom for there

to be a ceremony of betrothal before the marriage.
Often the marriage is not celebrated for two or three
years afterwards, the custom thereby resembling that of
the Early Church.   But let it not be supposed that the
betrothal is merely an exchange of promises whose
value depends entirely on the good faith of the con-
tracting parties.   The engagement is a much more
solemn affair, and if it is not recognized by the law of
the state it is recognized by the law of nature.   And so
a ceremony took place under the presidency of Pastor
Andresen at which Hulda and her lover were betrothed.
There was not a minister of religion at Dal, nor in any
of the neighbouring gaards.   In Norway there are
certain localities, called "Sunday towns," where the
parsonage or "proestegjelb" is situated.   There the
chief families of the parish assemble for service.

Dal, it is true, possessed a chapel, but the minister
only went there when asked, and for ceremonies that
were not public but private.   Mœl is not far away.   It
was hardly half a local mile—that is about three
English miles—from Dal to the end of Lake Tinn ; and
Pastor Andresen was an obliging man and a good
walker.   He was asked to perform the ceremony in his
twofold capacity of minister and friend of the Hansen
family whom he had known for many years.   He had
seen Hulda and Joel grow up, and had loved them as
he loved "the young sea wolf," Ole Kamp.   Nothing
could give him greater pleasure than this marriage,
which would cause the whole valley of Vestfjorddal to
keep holiday.   And so Pastor Andresen took his little
ruff, his crape bands, and his service-book, and set out
in the morning—a rainy one as it proved.   He arrived

accompanied by Joel, who had gone to meet him half-way. It need not be said how cordially he was received by Dame Hansen ; the best room on the ground floor was assigned to him, strewn with fresh branches of the juniper perfuming it as if it were a chapel.

Early next morning the little church of Dal was opened. There, before the pastor and on his service-book in the presence of a few friends and neighbours, Ole swore to marry Hulda, and Hulda swore to marry Ole when he returned from the last voyage he intended going. A year to wait is a long time, but it matters little when the betrothed are sure of each other. But Ole could not without some serious reason repudiate his promise ; nor could Hulda betray the trust she had sworn to keep. And if Ole had not gone away a few days afterwards, he would have been able to exercise the privileges that had been given him : to visit the girl when he chose, to write to her when he pleased, to accompany her arm-in-arm on her walks, even in the absence of her people, and to be preferred before all others as her partner in all dances and ceremonies.

But Ole Kamp had to be off to Bergen. The *Viking* started for the Newfoundland fisheries, and Hulda could do nothing but wait for the letters which her betrothed had promised to send her by every mail. And the letters did not fail her ; they brought a little gladness to the house which had become a somewhat miserable one since his departure. The voyage was prosperous, the fishing was abundant, the profits were large. And at the end of every letter Ole spoke of a certain secret and of a fortune which it would give him. Hulda would have been glad to know what this secret was, and so would Dame Hansen, for reasons that may be easily imagined.

The dame had become more and more gloomy, anxious and reserved. And a something happened which she did not mention to her children, which considerably increased her anxiety.

Three days after the arrival of the last letter from Ole, on the 19th of April, she was returning alone from the saw-mill where she had been to order a sack of shavings from overseer Lengling. Just as she reached the door of the house, she was accosted by a man who was a stranger in the district.

" You are Dame Hansen ? " asked the man.

" Yes," she replied, " but I do not know you."

" Oh ! that doesn't matter," said the man ; " I came this morning from Drammen, and am going back there."

" From Drammen ? " said the dame quickly.

" Do you know a Mr. Sandgoist who lives there ? "

" Mr. Sandgoist ! " said the dame, her face turning pale at the name.   " Yes—I know him."

" Well, when Mr. Sandgoist heard I was coming to Dal he told me to ask how you were."

" And—nothing else ? "

" Nothing ; except that he would probably come and see you next month.   Good evening, Dame Hansen ! "

CHAPTER V.

HULDA had been much concerned at this persistence
of Ole in always speaking in his letters of the fortune
he was to find when he returned. On what was this
expectation founded? Hulda could not divine, and
she longed to know. Such natural impatience was
excusable. Was it idle curiosity on her part? Not at
all. The secret affected her more than a little. Not
that she was ambitious, nor that her visions of the future
ever rose to what might be called wealth. Ole's love
was enough for her, and would always be enough for
her. If fortune came, she would welcome it without
extravagant joy; if it did not come, she would dispense
with it without extravagant grief.

This was exactly what Hulda said to Joel the day
after Ole's last letter had reached Dal. They thought
the same about this as about everything else; though
Joel added, " You must be hiding something from me."

" I—hiding something ? "

" Yes ! That Ole should go away without telling you
a little of his secret is incredible ! "

" Did he say anything to you about it ? "

" No, but I am not you. I am not Ole's betrothed."

" You are almost," said the girl. " If any accident
happens to him, if he does not return from this voyage,
your grief will be much the same as mine."

" Ah ! sister," answered Joel, " you must not have

such ideas! Ole not to come back from his last
voyage! Are you talking seriously, Hulda?"

"No, perhaps not. And yet I do not know—I
cannot help certain presentiments—horrible dreams—"

"Dreams, sister, are only dreams."

"Perhaps, but where do they come from?"

"From ourselves, and not from on high. You are
afraid, and your fear haunts your sleep. Besides, it is
nearly always so when you wish for something, and
the time comes near when your wishes are to be
realized."

"I know that."

"Really, I thought you were more resolute, more
energetic. You have just had a letter in which Ole tells
you that the *Viking* will be here before the month is out,
and you take such things as that into your head!"

"No—into my heart, Joel!"

"And here we are at the 19th April. Ole ought to
be here between the 15th and 20th of May; and it is
not too soon to begin preparing for your wedding."

"Do you think so, Joel?"

"Of course, I think so. I think you have delayed too
long! Think about it! A wedding that will bring
happiness, not only to us, but to all the neighbouring
gaards. I expect it will be something very grand, and
I am going to get things in order."

And a wedding is not a trifling matter in Norway in
general, and Tellemarken in particular. And it could
not pass without considerable fuss.

It followed, then, that Joel went that very day to
have some conversation with his mother about it. It so
happened that only a few minutes before Dame Hansen

had been so greatly flurried by the meeting with the
man who told her of Mr. Sandgoist's approaching visit.
She had gone to her seat in the armchair in the large
room, and there absorbed in her thoughts, was mechanically turning her wheel.

Joel saw at once that his mother was more disturbed
than usual ; but as she invariably said "it was nothing"
when they asked her about herself, Joel thought it best
to speak only of Hulda's marriage.

"Mother," said she, "you know we have learnt from
Ole's last letter that he will probably return to Tellemarken in a few weeks." .

"Let us hope so," answered the dame, "and may
nothing delay him ! "

"Do you see any inconvenience in our fixing the
25th of May for the wedding ? "

"None, if Hulda consents."

"Her consent is already given. And now, mother, I
want to know if you are going to do things well on the
occasion ? "

"What do you mean by doing things well ? " asked
the dame, without lifting her eyes from the wheel.

"I mean that the ceremony should be worthy of our
position in the bailiwick. We ought to invite our ac-
quaintances, for if the house is not large enough for
our guests there is not a neighbour that will not entertain them for us."

"Who are these guests, Joel ? "

"Well, we ought, I think, to invite all our friends from
Mœl, Tiness, and Bamble. I dare say that the presence
of Messrs. Help Brothers, the shipowners of Bergen,
would be an honour to the family, and with your

consent, be it understood, I should ask them to spend
a day at Dal. They are very good fellows, and they
are fond of Ole, and I am sure they would accept."

"Is it so necessary," asked the dame, "to treat this
marriage as of so much importance ?"

"I think so, mother, and it seems to me to be to the
interest of the inn at Dal which has not gone down, as
far as I am aware, since father's death."

"No—Joel—no!"

"Is it not our duty to maintain it, at least, in the
state he left it ? And so I think it wise to make a
little fuss about my sister's marriage."

"Be it so, Joel."

"On the other hand, is it not about time that Hulda
began to get her things ready, so that there should be
no delay ? What do you say ?"

"That Hulda and you can do what is necessary."

Perhaps it may be thought that Joel was in somewhat
of a hurry, and that it would have been more reasonable
to have waited for Ole's return to fix the wedding-day
and begin preparing for it. But as he said, what had to
be done might as well be done ; and it would at least
give Hulda something better to think about in busying
herself with the thousand details that such a ceremony
requires. It was important that she should not give
way to her presentiments, which nothing at present
justified, and to keep her from being overcome by them.

At the outset it was necessary to fix on a maid of
honour. But there was no difficulty in that. The
choice was already made—no other than the amiable
young lady of Bamble, Hulda's intimate friend. Her
father, farmer Helmboë, worked one of the most im-

portant gaards in the province. He was comfortably off ; and for a long time he had appreciated Joel, while his daughter had appreciated him no less. It was, therefore, not unlikely that in the good time coming, after Siegfrid had given her services to Hulda, Hulda would have to give hers to Siegfrid ; for in Norway such agreeable functions are generally reserved for married women. It was, therefore, rather a stooping for Joel's good that Siegfrid Helmboë was to act for Hulda Hansen.

It was an important question, for the betrothed as well as for the maid of honour, what they were to wear on the day of the ceremony. Siegfrid was a beautiful blonde of eighteen, and had quite made up her mind to appear to the best advantage. She had been written to by her friend Hulda—Joel had undertaken to deliver the letter into her own hands—and had set to work without losing a moment on a certain corsage on which the embroidery in regular patterns was to fit her like a coat of enamel. There was to be a skirt covering a series of petticoats, the number of which was to be in proportion to Siegfrid's fortune, but without detracting from the graces of her figure. With regard to the jewellery it would be a difficult matter to choose the central plate of the collar of silver filagree and pearls, the buckle of the corsage in gilded silver or copper, the heart-shaped pendants with the movable disks, the double buttons to fasten the shirt collar, the linen belt or the red silk one, from which hung the four rows of chains, the rings with the little tassels that harmoniously jingle, the earrings and the bracelets in pierced silver ; in short, all the rustic jewellery in which, to tell the truth, the gold is of the thinnest leaf, the silver mostly tin, the work mostly stamped, the pearls blown glass, and the diamonds quartz! But still the combination must please the eye. And that it should do so, Siegfrid did not hesitate to visit the ample stores of Mr. Bennett at Christiania to make her purchases. Her father did not object. Far from it! The excellent man let his daughter do as she liked, and Siegfrid was reasonable enough not to run her father's purse quite dry. The one thing, above all things necessary, was that on the eventful day Joel should find her looking her best.

Hulda was hardly less put about. Fashion is pitiless, and gives immense trouble in choosing a bridal dress. Hulda had to abandon the long plaits, which escaped from her girl's cap, and the high belt. She would no longer wear the neckerchiefs which Ole had given her when he went away ; nor the cord from which hung the little bags of embroidered leather in which are kept the short-handled spoon, the knife, the fork, and the needle-case—which a woman is likely to have in constant use in the house.

No! on the day of the wedding Hulda's hair would float freely on her shoulders, and it was so abundant that there would be no necessity to work in with it any of the flax wisps as many Norwegian brides have to do. For her clothes, as for her jewellery, Hulda would have to trust to her mother's wardrobe, for the elements of the bridal toilette are transmitted from wedding to wedding in every generation of the family. Each time there re-appear the doublet of gold embroidery, the velvet belt, the silk skirt, plain or speckled, the wadmel stockings, the chain of gold, the horn and the crown—that famous Scandinavian crown kept in the very best coffer, made

of magnificent gilded pasteboard relieved by bosses, and
spangled with stars garlanded in foliage, the equivalent
of the orange blossoms of the other countries of Europe.
One thing was certain, and that was that this radiant
nimbus with its delicate filagree, its jingling pendants,
and its trinkets of coloured glass would make a charming
frame for the pretty face of Hulda Hansen. The
"crowned wife," as they say, would do honour to her
husband. And he would be worthy of her in his
gorgeous wedding clothes—short jacket with silver
buttons close together, highly starched shirt collar,
bordered waistcoat braided with silk, tight breeches
fastened at the knee with clumps of flossy flax, soft felt
yellowish boots ; and at his belt in its leather sheath
the Scandinavian knife, the "dol knif" which no true
Norwegian is ever without. And thus in one way or
another there was plenty to do, and only a few weeks to
do it in if it was all to be finished by Ole's return. If
Ole arrived a little earlier than he said and Hulda was
not ready, Hulda would not complain—nor would Ole.

It was in these different ways that there passed the last
weeks of April and the first weeks of May. On his
part, Joel had himself issued his invitations, taking
advantage of his employment as guide which then
left him some leisure. It seemed that he had a good
many friends at Bamble, for he went there very often,
and though he had not gone to Bergen to invite Messrs.
Help Brothers, he had written to them, and, as he
expected, the honest shipowners had cordially accepted
the invitation to be present at the wedding of Ole Kamp,
the young captain of the *Viking*.

The 15th May came, and from day to day they

expected to see the captain descend from his carriole, open the door, and shout in his cheery voice,—

"Here I am!"

A little patience was wanted—that was all. Everything was ready. Siegfrid, on her part, only wanted the signal to appear in all her splendour.

The 16th passed, so did the 17th, and there was no letter from Newfoundland.

"You need not be surprised," said Joel frequently, "a sailing ship may meet with delays. It is a long voyage from St. Pierre to Bergen. If the *Viking* were only a steamer and I were the engine, how I would send her along against wind and tide!"

Thus he spoke because he saw how Hulda's anxiety grew from day to day.

And the weather was bad in Tellemarken. Boisterous winds swept over the higher fjelds; and the winds came from the west, from America.

"They ought to be fair for the *Viking!*" said the girl.

"Perhaps so," replied Joel. "But they are too strong, and the ship may have to lay to. You cannot always do what you like when you are at sea!"

"And you are not anxious, Joel?"

"No, Hulda, no! It is annoying, but it is only natural! I am not anxious, and really there is no reason for anxiety!"

On the 19th there arrived at the inn a tourist who needed a guide to take him through the mountains to Hardanger. Although he did not like leaving Hulda to herself, her brother could not refuse the offer. It would be an absence of forty-eight hours at the outside and Joel expected to find Ole when he came back. The truth is that he was getting very uneasy, and when he went away in the morning it was with a heavy heart.

At one o'clock in the afternoon of the day after, there came a knock at the inn door.

"Can that be Ole?" exclaimed Hulda.

She ran to the door.

On the threshold stood a man in a travelling cloak, perched on the seat of the carriole. His face was unknown to her.

CHAPTER VI.

" Does this inn belong to Dame Hansen ? "

" Yes, sir," answered Hulda.

" Is Dame Hansen there ? "

" No ; but she will be back soon."

" Immediately ? "

" At once. If you have anything to say to her—"

" Not at all. I have nothing to say to her."

" Do you want a room ? "

" Yes ; the best in the house."

" Are we to get dinner for you ? "

" As quickly as possible, and let me have the best you can give me."

Such was what passed between Hulda and the traveller before he descended from the carriole which had brought him into the heart of Tellemarken across the forests, lakes, and valleys of central Norway.

We know the carriole, that engine of locomotion, which the Scandinavians particularly affect. Two long shafts between which goes the horse, square of shoulder, yellowish of skin, striped like a mule, driven by a simple cord bit, passed not through his mouth but over his nose ; two large slender wheels whose axle has no springs, and supports a small coloured box hardly big enough for one—no head, no splash board, no step— behind the box a little plate on which is perched the skydskarl. The whole resembles an enormous spider,

whose double web is formed by the wheels. With this
rudimentary machine stages of from nine to twelve miles
are done without much fatigue.

At a sign from the traveller, the boy came and held
the horse. Then the rider rose, shook himself, and got
down not without an effort or two, which provoked a
few outbursts of ill-temper.

" You can put up the carriole ? " asked he in a gruff
tone as he stepped on the threshold.

" Yes, sir," answered Hulda.

" And give my horse something to eat."

" I'll have him put in the stable."

" Let him be taken care of."

" It shall be done. May I ask you if you are going to
stay a few days at Dal ? "

"I don't know."

The carriole and horse were taken to a little shed
built in the enclosure under the fruit trees at the foot of
the mountain. This was the only stable there was at
the inn, but it was enough.

A few minutes afterwards the traveller was installed in
the best room as he had requested. Then, after divesting
himself of his great coat, he began to warm his hands at
a good fire of dry wood that he had had lighted. Meanwhile, in order to please him, Hulda had ordered the piga
to get ready the best dinner she could. This piga was a
strong girl of the district who, during the summer season,
helped in the kitchen and in the heavy work of the
house.

The new arrival was still a strong man, although he
was over sixty. Thin, slightly bent, of middle height,
with bony head, smooth face, pointed nose, little eyes

with piercing look behind the large spectacles, a forehead
generally wrinkled with a frown, and lips too thin to let
kind words escape—he had the appearance of a pawn-
broker or usurer. Hulda felt that the traveller brought
no good to the house.

That he was a Norwegian was evident, but he had
assimilated all the vulgarity of the Scandinavian type.
His dress comprised a low hat with large brim, a coat
of whitish cloth, a double-breasted waistcoat, breeches
fastened at the knee by a silk strap, and over all a
sort of brown pelisse lined with sheepskin, necessitated
by the coldness of the nights in Tellemarken.

Hulda had not asked him for his name. But she
would soon know it as he would have to write it in the
day-book of the inn.

Dame Hansen now came back. Her daughter told
her a traveller had arrived and asked for the best dinner
and the best room she could give him. She did not
know if he was going to stay long as he had not told her.

"Did he not give his name?"

"No, mother."

"Nor where he came from?"

"No."

"It is some tourist, no doubt. It is a pity Joel is not
here to wait on him. What shall we do if he wants a
guide?"

"I do not know about his being a tourist," said Hulda.
"He is an oldish man."

"If he is not a tourist, what does he want at Dal?" said
the dame in a tone that seemed to betray some anxiety.

Hulda could not answer this question, for the traveller
had told her nothing of his plans.

An hour after his arrival the man entered the large room which adjoined his bedroom. On seeing Dame Hansen, he stopped for a moment at the door.

Evidently he was as unknown to his hostess as his hostess was to him. He came towards her, and after looking at her through his spectacles, said,—

"Dame Hansen, I believe?" without even touching his hat which remained on his head.

"Yes, sir," said the dame, like her daughter. And in the man's presence she felt uneasy.

"Are you really Dame Hansen of Dal?"

"Certainly, sir; have you anything particular to say to me?"

"Nothing. I only wished to make your acquaintance. Am I not your guest? And now will you let me have dinner as soon as possible?"

"Your dinner is ready," said Hulda. "Will you go into the dining-room?"

"I will."

And so saying the traveller walked towards the door that Hulda showed him, and a moment afterwards was seated near the window at a little table properly laid.

The dinner was certainly good. No tourist—not even the most difficult to please—could have found fault with it. But the diner spared neither signs nor sounds of disapproval—signs chiefly, for he seemed anything but talkative. Perhaps it was his bad digestion, perhaps it was his bad disposition which made him so difficult to please. The soup with cherries and gooseberries only half satisfied him, although it was excellent. He only touched with his lips the salmon and pickled herrings.

The plain boiled ham and the tasty half-fowl seemed not to please him. It was only with his bottle of St. Julien and half-bottle of champagne that he showed himself content, and that was because they came unmistakably from France. It follows, therefore, that when the traveller had finished he had not a single "tack for mad" for his hostess. After dinner this disagreeable visitor lighted his pipe, and went for a walk along the bank of the Maan.

He soon came back. He never lost sight of the house. It seemed as though he was making notes of all its sides, its plan, section, elevation, as if he were calculating its value. He counted the doors and the windows. Then he approached the beams laid horizontally along the base of the house, and tried them with his dolknif, as if to ascertain the quality of the wood and its state of preservation. Was he reckoning what the inn was worth? Was he going to buy what was not for sale? It seemed very strange. Then after he had finished with the house he attacked the enclosure and counted the trees and bushes. Then he measured the two sides of a ditch he had paced, and then the movement of the pencil in his note-book showed that he multiplied the figures together.

And all the time he nodded his head and scowled and frowned, and uttered a series of anything but approving "hums!" While this was going on, Dame Hansen and her daughter watched him through the room window. What strange customer had they to do with? What was the object of the journey of this maniac? It was indeed a pity that Joel was away if this man was going to stay at the inn all night.

" Suppose he is a madman ? " asked Hulda.

" A madman ?   No," answered Dame Hansen, "·but he is a very strange man."

" It is annoying that we do not know who he is."

" Before he comes in put the visitors' book in his room."

" Yes, mother."

" Perhaps he will sign his name in it ! "

By eight o'clock the night had become dark.   A gentle rain began to fall, filling the valley with a mist, which rose half up the mountains.   The weather was not inviting for a walk, but the visitor went away up the footpath to the sawmill and returned to the inn and asked for a glass of brandy.   Then, without saying a word, without even wishing a good-night, he took the wooden candlestick and lighted taper, entered his room, locked the door, and nothing more was heard of him for the night.

The skydskarl had simply taken his quarters in the stable, and there between the shafts of the carriole he already slept in company with the yellow horse, quite oblivious of the storm.

Next day the dame and her daughter were up with the dawn.   No sound came from the room where the traveller still slept.   A little after nine o'clock he came into the large room, looking even more surly than the evening before, complaining of the bed being hard, and of the noise in the house which had awoke him—and saying good-morning to nobody.   Then he opened the door and went out to look at the sky.

· The weather was not promising.   A strong wind swept the summit of Gousta, now hidden in mist, and

blew across the valley in violent squalls. The traveller
did not risk going out. But he did not waste his time.
Lighting his pipe he prowled about the inn prying into
its internal arrangements; he visited the different rooms,
examined the furniture, opened the presses and cup-
boards with as little ceremony as if he had been at
home. He seemed to be a broker's man intent on an
inventory. Most assuredly he was a mysterious man,
and his proceedings were more than suspicious.

Then he came and sat himself down in the big armchair in the large room; and in a rude peremptory
voice asked Dame Hansen a few questions. How long
had the inn been built? Was it built by her husband
or did he succeed to it? Had it been repaired? What
was the size of the enclosure and the sœter that went
with it? Was it well patronized and of good reputation? How many tourists visited it on the average
during the season? How long did they stay? &c., &c.

Evidently the traveller had taken no notice of the
book which had been placed in his room the night
before; for if he had seen it he would not have asked
this last question. In fact the book was where Hulda
had put it the night before, and the traveller's name did
not appear in it.

"Sir," said Dame Hansen, "I do not understand how
or why these things can interest you. But if you wish
to know what business we do, nothing is easier. You
have only to consult the day-book of the inn. I should
like you to enter your name in it as is usual—"

"My name? Certainly I will enter my name! I
will enter it when I bid you good-bye!"

"Are we to keep your room?"

" No," said the traveller rising. " I am going after breakfast so as to get back to Drammen to-morrow evening."

" To Drammen ? " said the dame.

" Yes ! so let me háve breakfast immediately."

" You live at Drammen ? "

"Yes ! What is there so astonishing, if you please, in my living at Drammen ? "

So that after staying nearly a whole day at Dal, or rather in the inn, the traveller was going back without seeing anything of the country! He was going no farther ! Gousta, the Rjukanfos, the wonders of the valley of Vestfjorddal interested him not in the least ! It was not for pleasure, it was for business that he had left Drammen, where he lived, and he seemed to have no other object than to visit Dame Hansen's house in detail !

Hulda saw that her mother was greatly agitated. The dame went to the large armchair, and there, pushing back her wheel, sat motionless without saying a word.

The traveller had gone into the dining-room and was seated at the table.

With the breakfast, which was as carefully served as the dinner the previous night, he appeared just as dissatisfied, though he ate well and drank well and did not hurry himself. His attention seemed chiefly engaged on the value of the silver—a luxury among the country folks of Norway—a few spoons and forks which were handed down from father to son and kept as carefully as the family jewels.

Meanwhile the skydskarl prepared for the start. At

eleven o'clock the horse and carriole were at the inn door. The weather was not inviting. The sky was grey and stormy. Every now and then the rain drenched the windows and showered against the glass as if the drops were small shot. But the traveller under his thick skin-lined coat was not the man to bother himself about a squall. Breakfast over, he took a last glass of brandy, lighted his pipe, and put on his over-coat. Then he went into the large room and asked for his bill.

"I will get it for you," said Hulda, seating herself before a small desk.

"Be quick," said the traveller, "and meantime give me the book that I may enter my name."

Dame Hansen rose, went to fetch the book, and laid it on the large table.

The traveller took up the pen, looked at the dame over his spectacles, and then in large letters wrote his name and shut the book. As he did so Hulda brought him the bill. He took it, checked over the items, grumbled, and ran over the addition.

"Hum!" said he, "that is rather dear! Seven marks and a half for a bed and two meals."

"There are the skydskarl and the horse," said Hulda.

"Doesn't matter! I say it's dear! And I am not astonished that you do well here."

"You owe us nothing, sir," said the dame in a troubled voice.

She had just opened the book, and read the name written therein, and she repeated, as she took the bill and tore it up,—

"You owe us nothing."

" So I thought," said the traveller.

And without saying good-morning any more than he had said good-evening when he came, he went out, and climbed into his carriole, as the boy jumped up behind ; and in a few minutes he had disappeared at the turn of the road.

When Hulda opened the book the name she found was—

" Sandgoist from Drammen."

CHAPTER VII.

IT was in the afternoon of the following day that Joel
returned to Dal. He had left the tourist with whom
he had gone as guide on the road to Hardanger.

Hulda, knowing he would come back across the slopes
of Gousta by the left bank of the Maan, had gone to
meet him where he would cross the impetuous river.
She, deep in thought, was sitting near the little wooden
gangway which served as a landing-stage for the ferry
boat. To her anxiety at the non-arrival of the *Viking*,
there was now added that of the visit of Sandgoist and
the dame's strange conduct towards him. Why, as
soon as she read his name, had she torn up his bill and
refused to take what was owing to her? Therein was
some great secret, of that there could be no doubt.

Hulda was recalled from her thoughts by the arrival
of Joel. She saw him as he came over the shoulder of
the mountain. Soon he appeared among the narrow
clearings where the trees in places had been burned or
felled. Then he vanished under the thick branching
pines, and the birches and beeches, with which the
ridges bristled. Soon he reached the opposite bank
and stepped into the ferry boat. A few strokes of the
oar sent him across the current, and then, jumping on
shore, he was beside his sister.

" Has Ole come ? " asked he.

It was of Ole that he first thought. But his question was left unanswered.

" No letter from him ? "

" None."

And Hulda burst into tears.

"Don't cry," said Joel, "don't cry. It isn't fair to me. I cannot bear to see you cry. Look here ! you say, no letter ! Evidently that looks a little strange ! But you need not despair yet. If you like I'll go to Bergen. I will find out. I will see Help Brothers. Perhaps they have news from Newfoundland. Why should not the *Viking* have put in at some port to repair damages or been driven in by the weather? We know there was a gale which lasted more than a week. Sometimes the vessels from Newfoundland put in to Iceland or the Faroes. That is what happened to Ole himself two years ago when he was in the *Strenna*. And the post doesn't come every day for people to write. I am telling you what I really think. Be quiet. If you make me cry what is to become of us ? "

" I cannot help it."

"Hulda ! Hulda ! Do not lose courage ! I assure you I have not given him up."

" Can I believe you, Joel ? "

"Yes, you can ! But to give you confidence shall I go to Bergen to-morrow or to-night ? "

" I do not want you to leave me ! No ! I do not want you to go," said Hulda, clinging to her brother as if he were all she had in the world.

They then started along the road to the inn. As well as he could Joel sheltered his sister against the rain. But the storm became so violent that they had to take refuge in the ferryman's hut a few hundred yards from the banks of the Maan.   There they had to wait till the storm somewhat abated, and then Joel felt that he must talk ; for the silence seemed so hopeless, that somehow it must be broken, even though the words might not be of hope.

"How is mother ?" said he.

"More miserable than ever."

"Has any one come while I have been away ?"

"Yes, a traveller who has gone again."

"Then there is no tourist at the inn and no one has asked for a guide ?"

"No, Joel."

"So much the better, for I had rather not leave you. Besides, if this weather continues, I am afraid we shall have hardly any tourists in Tellemarken this year."

"We are only in April."

"Quite so, but I have an idea that we shall not have a good season!   We shall see!   But, tell me, did your traveller go away yesterday ?"

"Yes, in the morning."

"And who was he ?"

"A man from Drammen, where he lives, of the name of Sandgoist."

"Sandgoist !"

"Do you know him ?"

"No," said Joel.

Hulda had already asked herself if she should tell her brother all that had happened at the inn while he was away.   When Joel learnt with what rudeness the man had behaved himself, how he seemed to have taken stock of the house and the furniture, and the way in which Dame Hansen had thought fit to treat him, what would he imagine? Would he not think that his mother had serious reasons for acting as she had done? What were these reasons? What could there be in common between her and Sandgoist? Therein certainly lay a secret that boded ill for the family! Joel would insist on knowing it, he would ask his mother; he would cross-examine her. Dame Hansen, never very communicative, always so averse to a scene, would keep her counsel as before. The state of affairs between her and her children would become worse than ever!

But ought the girl to keep it from Joel? a secret from him! Would it not be like a straw in the friendship of iron which bound them together. No! The friendship must never end! Hulda resolved to tell him everything.

"You never heard of this Sandgoist when you were at Drammen?" she asked.

"Never!"

"Well then, Joel, mother knew him, or at least knew his name."

"She knew Sandgoist?"

"Yes."

"But I never heard her mention his name!"

"She knew it, nevertheless, although she had never seen him till yesterday."

And Hulda then told her brother all that had happened while Sandgoist was at the inn, not forgetting the dame's curious proceedings when he left. She concluded her story with,—

"I think, Joel, you had better say nothing about it to our mother. You know her! It would make her still more unhappy. The future will probably explain the past. Would that Ole was given back to us and then, if any affliction is to befall, there would be three to share it."

Joel listened to his sister with profound attention. Yes! Between Dame Hansen and this Sandgoist there was a something which put one at the other's mercy! Could it be doubted that this man had come to make an inventory of the inn at Dal? Assuredly not! And the bill torn up as he left—which seemed so natural to him—what did that mean?

"You are right, Hulda," said Joel, "I will not speak to mother. Perhaps she will be sorry she has not confided in us. May it not be too late! She does suffer, poor woman! She is so contrary, and does not see that her children's hearts were made for her to pour her troubles into."

"She will understand it some day."

"Yes; and so we must wait. But meanwhile I do not see why we shouldn't try and find out who this man is. Perhaps Mr. Helmboë knows him? I will ask him the first time I go to Bamble, and if needful I will go on to Drammen. There it will not be difficult to learn what this man is, and what he does—"

"Nothing good, I am sure," said Hulda. "His face is a bad one, and he has an evil look. I shall be very much surprised if there is a generous heart under such a forbidding envelope."

"Never judge people by their appearance," said Joel. "I'll wager you would have found his face pleasant enough if you looked at it while you were in Ole's arms.—"

" My poor Ole ! " murmured the girl.

" He will come back, he is coming back, he is on the road," said Joel. " Have confidence, Hulda ! Ole is not far away now, and we are grumbling at his return, instead of waiting for it."

The rain had ceased. They left the hut and walked up the path to the inn.

" I'm off again to-morrow," said Joel.

" You are off again ?—"

" Yes, to-morrow."

" Already ? "

" I must go, Hulda. When I left Hardanger I was told by one of my comrades that a tourist was coming from the north by the high lands of the Rjukanfos, where he would arrive to-morrow."

" Who is the tourist ? "

" I don't know his name. But I must be there to bring him on to Dal."

" Then you must go, if you cannot get out of it," said Hulda, with a deep sigh.

" To-morrow at daybreak I shall be off. Will you be very sorry, Hulda ? "

" Yes. I am much more uneasy when you are away from me—even for a few hours."

" Well, this time I am not going alone."

" And who is going with you ? "

" You, sister, you ! You want a change, and I will take you with me."

" Thank you, Joel."

CHAPTER VIII.

AT dawn next day they left the inn. Nine miles from Dal to the celebrated waterfall and nine miles back was only a walk for Joel; but it would not do to overtax Hulda's strength. Joel, therefore, availed himself of the carriole belonging to overseer Lengling, which, like all these carrioles, had hardly room for two; but the box was big enough for Hulda and Joel; and, if the traveller was at the Rjukanfos, he could take the place of Joel, who could either return on foot or on the board behind.

It is a charming road from Dal to the falls, although the jolts it causes are plentiful. It is indeed more of a footpath than a road. Beams half squared are thrown across the tributaries of the Maan, forming small bridges every few hundred yards; but the Norwegian horse is accustomed to cross them with sure foot, and although the carriole has no springs, its long elastic shafts ease the joltings considerably.

It was a fine morning. Joel and Hulda went at a good pace over the verdant fields bathed on their left by the clear waters of the Maan. Thousands of birches shaded the road from the bright sunshine. The night mist hung in tears from the points of the long grass. On the right of the stream, six thousand feet above them, the many slopes of Gousta threw off into space an intense radiation of the light.

For an hour the carriole went along rapidly. The

rise at present was imperceptible. But soon the valley
began to close in, and the streams grew to be furious
torrents. The road became more winding, and it was
impossible to avoid all the irregularities of the ground.
There were places where the passage was really difficult,
and these Joel cleverly managed to get over. When
he was near, Hulda feared nothing; when the jolt was
very violent she clung to his arms. The freshness of
the morning tinged with colour the pretty face that had
been pale for so long.

But a greater height had to be reached. The valley
hardly yields a passage to the narrow course of the
Maan between its two high peaked walls. On the
neighbouring fields there were a score of isolated
houses, sœters or gaards abandoned in ruins, and
shepherds' huts lost under the birches and beeches.
Soon it was impossible to see the river which roared
along deep in the sonorous casing of rock. The scenery
became grander and wilder, and the picture enlarged
its frame up to the crest of the mountains.

After driving for two hours a sawmill was sighted by
the side of a fall, fifteen hundred feet high, used for
working its double wheel. Cascades of this height
are not rare in Vestfjorddal, but their volume is
inconsiderable, and hence the importance of the
Rjukanfos.

Joel and Hulda reached the sawmill and alighted.

"Half an hour's walk will not tire you too much?"
asked Joel.

"No, brother, I am not tired, and it will do me good
to walk a little."

"A little! Much—and uphill all the way!"

" I can lean on your arm, Joel."

The carriole had to be left here. It could not be taken up the difficult paths, the narrow passages, the slopes dotted with loose rocks, whose capricious forms shaded with trees or left unclothed showed that the fall was near, while a thick mist rose in the blue distance, the pulverized water of the Rjukan floating aloft in huge volutes.

Hulda and Joel followed a track well known to the guides, which took them down to the throat of the valley, amid the trees and bushes. In a few minutes they were seated on a rock carpeted with golden mosses almost in front of the fall. On that side this was the nearest they could get.

There the brother and sister would have found it difficult to hear each other had they spoken. But their thoughts were those which can be communicated without being formulated by the lips—but by the heart.

The volume of the Rjukan fall is enormous, its height is considerable, and its roar is great. Nine hundred feet above, the Maan finds its bed suddenly drop beneath it, just halfway between Lake Mjös up stream and Lake Tinn down stream. Nine hundred feet, that is to say, six times the height of Niagara, whose breadth, however, is three miles from the American to the Canadian bank.

The Rjukanfos has many curious aspects difficult of description. Even the painter could not render them satisfactorily. There are many natural wonders which must be seen if all their beauties are to be understood, and among them is this waterfall, the most famous on the continent of Europe.

And this a tourist was doing as he sat on the left bank of the Maan, watching the full height of the Rjukanfos from the nearest point.

Neither Joel nor his sister had yet seen him, although he was visible. This was not because of the distance, but because of an optical effect peculiar to mountain scenery, which always seems to dwarf things and make them appear farther away than they actually are.

At the moment the traveller had just got up, and was imprudently venturing on the rocky ridge which rounded the bed of the river as if it were a dome. Evidently he wished to see the two caves in the Rjukanfos, one to the left full of the foaming waters, the other to the right thick with the dense vapour. Perhaps he was looking for a third cavity lower down, midway in the fall which would explain why the Rjukan, after being engulphed, burst forth again at intervals in full tumultuous flood and covered everything with the spray as though a mine had been sprung beneath it.

The tourist advanced along the ridge which, stony and slippery, bare of root, or clump, or vegetation, bears the name of the Maristien. He knew not, evidently, the legend which has made the ridge famous : One day Eystein sought to rejoin by this dangerous road the fair Mary of Vestfjorddal. On the other side his betrothed stretched her hands towards him. Suddenly he missed his footing, fell, slipped, could not stop himself on the rocks which are smooth as ice, vanished into the gulf, and the Maan never yet gave up his corpse.

That is what happened to Eystein ; was it going to happen to the daring man who was now on the slopes of the Rjukanfos ?

E

It was to be feared so. And, in fact, he saw his
danger, but it was too late. Suddenly he slipped, and
shouted, and rolled about twenty yards, and only just
had time to catch hold of a projecting rock on the brink
of the abyss.

Joel and Hulda had not yet seen him, but they heard
him.

"What was that?" asked Joel as he rose.

"A shout," said Hulda.

"Yes ; a shout of distress!"

"Where did it come from?"

"Listen."

They looked to the right, to the left, of the fall : they
could see nothing. But they had heard the words "Here!
here!" in one of the moments of silence between each
leap of the Rjukanfos.

Again they heard the shout.

"Joel," said Hulda, "there is some traveller in danger
who wants help. You must go to him."

"Yes, and he is not far off. But where is he? I see
nothing."

Hulda climbed the slope behind the rock on which
they had been sitting, clinging to the little bushes which
hereabouts grow on the left bank of the Maan.

"Joel!" she exclaimed.

"Do you see him?"

"There! There!"

And Hulda pointed to the man hanging over the gulf.
If his foot, thrust against the tiny ledge, failed him, if he
slipped a little lower, if vertigo attacked him, he was
lost!

"We must save him," said Hulda.

"Yes, we must," said Joel. "If we keep cool we can get to him."

Joel gave a long, loud shout. He was heard by the traveller, who turned his head towards him. Then for an instant or two he thought over which was the quickest and safest way of getting the man out of danger.

"Hulda," he said, "you are not afraid?"

"No."

"You know the Maristien well?"

"I have been over it many times."

"Well, go round over the ridge and get as near the traveller as you can. Then slip slowly down to him and catch hold of his hand as tight as you can. But don't let him try to pull himself up or vertigo will attack dim, and he will drag you down with him, and you will be lost!"

"And what are you going to do?"

"While you are going over the top, I'll go along the bottom by the side of the Maan. I'll be there as soon as you, and if you slip over I will catch you both."

Then with a resounding shout, during a fresh silence in the roar of the Rjukanfos, Joel told the traveller,—

"Do not move! Wait! We are coming to you!"

Hulda had already disappeared behind the high bushes of the slope, so as to descend the other ridge of the Maristien from the side.

Joel did not stop to see the brave girl who came into view again as she reached the last trees.

On this part, at the peril of his life, he began to climb slowly along the declivity of the rounded boss which encircles the Rjukanfos. What astonishing coolness, what sureness of foot and hand he needed to skirt the abyss whose walls were wet with the spray of the cataract !

Parallel to him, but separated from him by a hundred feet above, Hulda advanced obliquely so as to reach most easily the place where the traveller was clinging motionless.   In the position she occupied her face could not be seen, as it was turned away from the fall.

Joel arrived below her, and stopped.   Then, planting his feet firmly in a cleft in the rock, he shouted,—

" Sir ! "

The traveller turned his head.

" Sir," said Joel, "don't move, wait a bit, and hold tight."

" All right, I'll hold on, my friend," said he in a voice that made Joel feel much relieved.   "If I hadn't held on, I should have been at the bottom of the Rjukanfos a quarter of an hour ago."

" My sister will come down to you," continued Joel. " She will take hold of your hand.   But don't try to pull yourself up ! and don't move."

" No more than a rock would," said the traveller.

Already Hulda had begun to slip down, seeking the least slippery parts of the slope, thrusting her feet in the cracks so as to get a firm footing, her head as clear as that of any of the daughters of Tellemarken accustomed to scale the ridges of the fjelds.

And as Joel had shouted, so shouted she,—

" Hold on, sir."

" Yes, I'll hold on—and I'll hold on, I assure you, as long as I can."

There was no lack of advice.   It came to him from above and below.

" Above all things, don't you feel afraid ! " said Hulda.

" My sister will come down to you."

Page 68.

"I'm not afraid."

"We'll save you!" shouted Joel.

"I hope so; for, by Saint Olaf, I can't save myself."

Evidently the traveller had kept his coolness pretty well. But when he fell his arms and legs would probably fail him, and all he could do now was to hang on to the little ledge which kept him from the abyss.

Hulda all the time was getting down to him, and at last she reached him. Then, having thrust her foot against a projection in the rock, she grasped his hand.

The traveller tried to raise himself a little.

"Don't move, sir! Don't move!" said she; "you will drag me with you, and I shall not be strong enough to hold you back. You must wait for my brother! When he has placed himself between us and the Rjukan-fos, you can try to pull yourself up, so as to—"

"Pull myself up, my brave girl! That is easier said than done, and I am afraid it will be very difficult—"

"Are you hurt, sir?"

"Hum! Nothing broken, nothing dislocated, but I have a splendid abrasion all down my leg."

Joel was then about twenty feet from Hulda and the traveller—below them. The curving of the slope prevented his going straight towards them, and he had now to make his way up the rounded surface. This was the most difficult and dangerous part of his attempt. It was at the risk of his life.

"Not a movement, Hulda!" said he for the last time; "if you slip, and I am not in a position to stop you, we are all done for."

"Never fear," said Hulda, "look after yourself, and may Heaven help you!"

Joel began to hoist himself on his stomach, dragging himself along in reptilian style. Twice or thrice he felt that all support would fail him, but thanks to his skill he managed to get up to the traveller, who was a man well on in years, but of healthy complexion, with a fine, pleasant, goodnatured-looking face. Joel thought to have found some young dare-devil.

"You have done a very foolish thing, sir," said he, as he crouched down to regain his breath.

"Foolish!" said the traveller. "Say rather, absurd!"

"You have risked your life!"

"And made you risk yours!"

"Oh! mine!—that is all in my trade!"

Then as he stood up, he continued,—

"Now we must get up the ridge, but the worst is over!"

"Oh! the worst is over!"

"Yes, sir! that was to get to you. We have only to work up along a much gentler slope."

"Don't reckon too much on me, my boy! My leg will not be of much use to me now for some days, perhaps."

"Try to get up!"

"Willingly—with your help."

"You take my sister's hand, and I will help you and push you by the waist."

"Well, my friends, I trust to you. You have been thinking how to get me out, and it's your business."

They did as Joel had said—cautiously. If the mounting of the ridge was not without a certain amount of danger, the three managed it quicker and better than they hoped. The traveller was suffering only from a bad abrasion, not from a sprain or a fracture, and he made better use of his legs than he expected. Ten minutes afterwards they were safe beyond the Maristien.

There they could rest beneath the first pine-trees which bordered the upper fjeld of the Rjukanfos. But Joel required him to make a further effort. He wished to reach a hut under the trees a little behind the rock at which his sister and he had stopped when they arrived at the fall. The traveller tried to make the necessary effort, and succeeded; helped on one side by Hulda, and on the other by Joel, he reached the door of the hut.

" Go in, sir," said the girl, "and then you can rest for a minute."

" Will the minute be a quarter of an hour ? "

" Yes, and then you must come with us to Dal."

" To Dal—but it is to Dal I want to go."

" Are you the tourist from the north," asked Joel, " of whom I was told at Hardanger ? "

" Exactly."

" Well, you didn't take the best road ! "

" So I think."

" And if I had known what was going to happen I should have met you on the other side of the Rjukanfos ! "

" That's a good idea ! And you would have spared me an imprudence unpardonable at my age."

" At every age, sir," said Hulda.

They entered the hut where they found a peasant family, consisting of the father and two daughters, who rose and welcomed them warmly.

Joel then ascertained that the traveller had only grazed his leg badly a little below the knee. This would necessitate a week's rest, but there was nothing dislocated or broken, and the bone had not been touched.

Excellent milk, abundant strawberries, and a little brown bread were offered and accepted. Joel did not conceal a very hearty appetite, and, if Hulda ate little, the traveller did his best to keep level with her brother.

"Really," said he, "that performance knocked a hole in my stomach! But I willingly admit that it was most imprudent to take the Maristien in that way! Wanting to play the part of the unfortunate Eystein when I might be his father—or his grandfather."

"Then you know the legend?" said Hulda.

"Don't I know it! My nurse used to get me to sleep with it, singing it to me at that happy age when I still had a nurse! Yes, I know it, my brave girl, and that makes me all the more guilty. Now, my friends, Dal is rather a long way for an invalid like me! How are you going to take me there?"

"Don't be uneasy, sir," said Joel, "our carriole is at the bottom of the footpath; you have only three hundred yards to go."

"Hum! Three hundred yards!"

"Downhill," said Hulda.

"Oh! if it is downhill that will be all right, and one arm will be enough for me."

"And why not two," asked Joel, "when we have four at your service?"

"In for two, in for four! That will not cost me too much, will it?"

"It will not cost you anything."

"So ! At least more thanks for each arm ; and that reminds me I have not yet thanked you—"

"For what ? " asked Joel.

"Simply that you saved my life at the risk of your own."

"Are you ready ? " said Hulda, rising to avoid being complimented.

"What ? I wish I was."

And then the traveller paid the small charge of the peasants in the hut ; and then, helped a little by Hulda and a good deal by Joel, he began to descend the winding footpath which leads down to the bank of the Maan and joins the road to Dal.

This was not done without many an " Oh ! Oh !" which invariably ended in a shout of laughter. At last the sawmill was reached, and Joel set to work getting ready the carriole.

Five minutes afterwards the traveller was installed in the carriage with the girl near him.

" And you ? " asked he of Joel, "it seems to me that I have taken your place."

" A place I willingly give you."

" But perhaps by squeezing—"

" No—no—I have my legs, sir, my guide's legs. They are better than wheels—"

" First-rate ones—my boy—first-rate ones ! "

They set out along the road which gradually nears the Maan. Joel walked at the horse's head and guided him by the bridle so as to avoid as much jolting as possible. The return was made in high spirits—at least on the part of the traveller. He chatted away like an old friend of the Hansen family. Before the journey

was over the brother and sister were calling him " Mr.
Sylvius," and Mr. Sylvius was addressing them as Hulda
and Joel as if he had known them for years.

About four o'clock the little clock tower of Dal
appeared above the trees of the hamlet, and a few
minutes afterwards the horse stopped before the inn.
The traveller alighted not without difficulty. Dame
Hansen was at the door to receive him, and, although he
did not ask for the best room in the house, it was given
him nevertheless.

CHAPTER IX.

SYLVIUS HOG—that was the name which that evening was inscribed in the visitors' book immediately below that of Sandgoist.   As strong a contrast between the two names as between the two men !   Nothing had they in common.   Generosity on the one side, greed on the other ; one all good-nature, the other all meanness and selfishness.

Sylvius Hog was nearly sixty, although he did not look so old ; tall, upright, well built, sound in mind and body.   You liked him from the very first, with his handsome, good-natured face, beardless, but set off well by the grey hair which was somewhat long.   His eyes, like his lips, seemed to be ever smiling ; in his massive forehead the noblest thoughts could circulate without difficulty, in his capacious chest his heart could beat at its ease.   To all these advantages he had an unfailing fund of good-humour, and a nature capable of every kindness and unselfishness.

Sylvius Hog of Christiania—that was all it said.   And not only was he known, appreciated, loved and honoured, in the Norwegian capital, but throughout the country —the Norwegian country be it understood ; for the sentiments people felt towards him were not the same in the other half of the Scandinavian kngdom—that is in Sweden—and for the following reason.

Sylvius Hog was professor of law at Christiania.

In other countries to be a lawyer, engineer, doctor, or merchant, is to occupy the higher ranks in the social scale. In Norway it is not so. To be a professor is to be at the summit.

If in Sweden there are four classes, the nobility, clergy, the middle class, and the peasants, there are only three in Norway, for there is no nobility. There is no representative of an aristocracy, not even an aristocracy of officials. In this privileged country, where no privileges exist, the officials are the servants of the public. In fact there is perfect social equality and no political distinction.

Sylvius Hog being one of the most considerable men in the country, it is not to be wondered at that he was a member of the Storthing. In this large assembly by his worth, as well as by the probity of his private and public life, he exercised an influence which far exceeded that of the peasant-deputies elected in such numbers by the two countries.

Since the constitution of 1814 it can be said with truth that Norway is a republic with the King of Sweden for president. Norway is very jealous of its prerogatives, and has known how to preserve its autonomy. The Storthing has nothing in common with the Swedish parliament ; and it can easily be understood that one of the most influential and patriotic of its members was not likely to be appreciated beyond the ideal frontier which separates Norway from Sweden.

So it was with Sylvius Hog. Of very independent character, and wanting for nothing, he had often refused to enter the ministry. A defender of all the rights of Norway, he was constantly and bitterly opposed to all

the encroachments of Sweden. And such is the moral
and political separation of the two countries, that the
King of Sweden—then Oscar XV.—after being crowned
at Stockholm, had to be crowned at Drontheim, the
ancient capital of Norway. Such is the rather jealous
caution of the Norwegians in business that the bank of
Christiania will not willingly receive the notes of the
bank of Stockholm ! Such is the division between the
two peoples, that the Swedish flag does not float over
the buildings or ships of Norway. In one the blue
bunting is traversed by a yellow cross, in the other the
cross is blue on a field of red.

Sylvius Hog was heart and soul for Norway. He
defended its interests on all occasions. In 1854, when
the Storthing discussed the question of having neither a
viceroy at the head of the country, nor even a governor,
he was one of those who took a foremost part in the
discussion and voted with the majority.

It is conceivable, therefore, that if he was not much
liked in the eastern kingdom, he was so in the western,
even in the remotest gaards. His name was familiar
throughout mountainous Norway, from Christiania to
the North Cape. Worthy of this genuine popularity,
no calumny had ever attacked the dignity of the
Christiania professor. He was a true Norwegian, but
a Norwegian of a lively temperament, with none of the
traditional phlegm of his countrymen, and more decided
in thought and action, as was witnessed by his prompt
movements, the ardour of his speech, and the vivacity
of his gestures.

Sylvius Hog had made no money out of public affairs,
and was only possessed of a modest competence.

Unselfish as he was he did not think of himself, but constantly he thought of others. And he turned up his nose at grandeur. To be a deputy was all his ambition; he wanted nothing beyond. At the time we speak of he was on a three months' holiday, recovering from the fatigues of a laborious year of legislative work. He had left Christiania six weeks before, intending to see the country about Drontheim, Hardanger, Tellemarken, and the district of Kongsberg, and Drammen. He wished to visit the provinces he had not yet seen, and make his tour one of study and amusement combined.

Sylvius Hog had already traversed a part of this country, and it was on his return from the northern bailiwicks, that he had gone to visit the famous fall which is one of the wonders of Tellemarken. After studying on the spot the plans of the railway from Drontheim to Christiania, he had asked for a guide to Dal, and arranged to meet him on the left bank of the Maan. But without waiting for him, and attracted by the scenery of the Maristien, he had ventured on the dangerous ridge.

It might have cost him his life. And had it not been for the coming of Joel and Hulda Hansen, his tour would have finished in the abyss of the Rjukanfos.

CHAPTER X.

In these Scandinavian countries the people are well
educated, not only in the towns, but in the country
places. The instruction goes beyond merely reading,
writing, and reckoning. The peasant learns with
pleasure. His intelligence is keen ; he interests himself in public affairs, and takes his share in political and
local matters. In the Storthing the peasant members
are in the majority, and sometimes they attend in the
costume of their province. They are justly noted for
their judgment, their good, practical sense, their com-
prehension—albeit a little slow—and above all for their
incorruptibility.

We need not be surprised, therefore, that the name of
Sylvius Hog was known throughout Norway, and
greeted with respect in this not very out-of-the-way spot
in Tellemarken.

And Dame Hansen, in receiving a guest so universally
esteemed, could not refrain from telling him how much
she was honoured at having him for a few days under
her roof.

"I don't know about the honour, Dame Hansen," said
Sylvius, "but I know it gives me a great deal of pleasure.
For a long time I have heard my pupils speak of this
hospitable hostelry at Dal. That is why I thought I
would stay here a week."

"Mr. Sylvius," said Hulda, "shall my brother go to Bamble for a doctor for you?"

"A doctor, my little Hulda! Do you want me to lose the use of my two legs?"

"Oh! Mr. Sylvius!"

"A doctor! Why not my friend Doctor Bock of Christiania? And all for a mere scratch!"

"But a scratch, if it is badly looked after," said Joel, "may become serious."

"Ah! Joel, will you tell me why you want it to become serious?"

"I don't want it to become serious, Mr. Sylvius, God help me!"

"Well, He will help you and me too, and all the house of Hansen, particularly if the gentle Hulda will look after me—"

"Certainly, sir."

"That will do, then? In four or five days there will be no trace of it! Besides, how can you keep ill in such a pleasant room as this? Where can one be better looked after than in this hostelry at Dal? And this splendid bed with its mottoes better than all the prescriptions of the faculty; and this delightful window opening on to the Maan, while the murmur of the water whispers in every corner of the room! And the perfume of the old trees with which all the house is scented! And the fine air, the mountain air, better than all the doctors. When you want him you have only to open the window, and there he is to cheer you up, and he never talks of dieting you!"

Gaily he rattled on, and with him it seemed as though a little happiness had also entered the dwelling. At least that is what the brother and sister thought, as they held each other's hands and listened, giving themselves over to the same feeling.

The professor had been taken into the room on the ground floor. There, half-lying in the large armchair, with his leg resting on a stool, he was attended to by Joel and Hulda. All he would have done was to have his leg bathed with cold water, that was all. And what else was necessary?

"Well, my friends," said he, "without you I should have seen the marvels of the Rjukanfos a little too near. I should have gone rolling down into the abyss like a stone, and added a new legend to the legend of the Maristien, and that without any excuse. My sweetheart was not waiting for me on the other side like the miserable Eystein!"

"And how sorry Mrs. Hog would have been!" said Hulda. "Nothing could ever have consoled her—"

"Mrs. Hog?" interrupted the professor. "Mrs. Hog would not have shed a tear!"

"Oh! Mr. Sylvius!"

"Not she! And for the very good reason that there is no Mrs. Hog! And I cannot even imagine what Mrs. Hog would have been like—fat or thin, stumpy or tall—"

"She would have been amiable, clever, and good, if she were your wife," said Hulda.

"Oh, indeed, Miss! Good! good! I believe you! I think she would!"

"But, on hearing of such a mishap, your relatives, sir—" said Joel.

"Relatives! I have hardly any, my boy! Of friends

it seems I have a certain number, without counting those I am going to make in Dame Hansen's house—and you have saved them the trouble of weeping for me. And now, can you let me stay here for a few days ? "

" For as many as you please, sir," said Hulda. " This room is yours."

" I intended to stay at Dal, as the tourists do, and make it a centre for exploring Tellemarken. I shall not explore it, or I shall explore it later on, that is all."

" Before the end of the week, sir," answered Joel, " I hope you will be on your legs again."

" And so do I."

" And then I will take you wherever you like in this district."

" We will see about it, Joel. We will talk about it again when this graze is better. I have still two months' holiday before me, and if I have to pass the whole time in Dame Hansen's inn I shall not complain. I must visit the valley of Vestfjorddal between the lakes, I must go up the Gousta, I must have another look at the Rjukanfos, for, although I nearly went into it, I hardly saw it—and I intend to see it."

" You shall see it again," said Hulda.

" And we shall see it together, if the dame will come with us. And—I think I had better send a line to Kate, my old nurse, and Fink, my old servant, at Christiania. They will be very uneasy if I don't send them any news, and I shall get a scolding. And now I have made my confession, strawberries and cream are very nice, and very refreshing, but they are not very substantial, and I should like to know what time you dine ? "

" That doesn't matter, sir."

"It matters a great deal! Do you think while I am staying here I am going to make myself miserable all alone in my room? No; I am going to have my meals with you and your mother, unless your mother objects."

Very naturally, Dame Hansen, when she heard of the traveller's request, did not object. It would be an honour for her to sit down to table with a member of the Storthing.

"So it is understood," said Hog, "we will take our meals together in the large room."

"Yes," answered Joel; "I have only to push in your armchair when dinner is ready."

"Good, Mr. Joel! And why not take me in in the carriole? No! with the help of your arm I'll get there. I have not had my leg taken off as far as I know."

"As you please," said Hulda; "but do not be rash when there is no need for it—or Joel will have to go for the doctor."

"Threats! Well, yes, I will be careful, and obey. And if you don't put me on sick allowance I shall be the most manageable of men. But are you not getting hungry?"

"We only want a quarter of an hour," said Hulda, "and you shall have some gooseberry soup, a Maan trout, a grouse that Joel brought from Hardanger yesterday, and a bottle of French wine."

"Thank you, my girl."

Hulda went out to look after the dinner and lay the table in the large room, while Joel took home the carriole to overseer Lengling.

Sylvius Hog was left alone. Of what could he be thinking, if it was not of this honest family of whom

he was at once the guest and the debtor? How could he
reward the services and attention of Hulda and Joel?
But he had no time to abandon himself to long reflections, for ten minutes afterwards he was seated in
the place of honour at the large table. The dinner was
excellent. It was worthy of the reputation of the inn,
and the professor ate it with good appetite.

The evening passed in conversation, in which Sylvius
Hog took the chief part. As Dame Hansen hardly
spoke, he addressed himself to the brother and sister.
The interest he had taken in them could not but increase.
So touching a friendship united them to each other, that
once or twice the professor was deeply affected. When
night closed in, he returned to his room, helped by Joel
and Hulda, and as soon as he lay down in the large bed
with the mottoes, he fell fast asleep.

In the morning Sylvius Hog awoke with the dawn,
and before any one had knocked at his door began to
think over what had passed.

"No," he said to himself, "I do not see how I am to
get out of it. I cannot let them rescue me, take care of
me, and cure me, and then ban them with a mere thank
you. I am under an obligation to Hulda and Joel that
is undeniable; but the service they have done is not
one we can pay for with money. On the other hand,
this family seems happy enough, and I don't see how I
can add to their happiness! Well, we must talk about
it, and while we are talking perhaps—"

For three or four days the professor had to keep his
leg upon the stool, and during the time he chatted
with his friends. Unfortunately there was a certain
reserve on the part of the brother and sister. Neither of

them cared to say anything about their mother, whose
cold, anxious demeanour the professor had noticed.
And owing to another sentiment of discretion they
hesitated to let him know anything of anxiety as to the
delay in Ole Kamp's return. In telling their guest
their troubles was there not a risk of spoiling his good-
humour?

"Perhaps," said Joel to his sister, "we are wrong in
not telling Mr. Sylvius. He is a sensible man, and by
his friends might be able to find out if they are anxious
about the *Viking* at the shipping office."

"You are right, Joel," answered Hulda, "I think we
had better tell him all; but wait till he is nearly well."

"Yes; and that will not be long," replied Joel.

In a week Sylvius Hog no longer needed assistance in
walking from his room, although he still limped a little.
He had got out so as to sit on one of the benches in
front of the house under the shadow of the trees.
Thence he could look away to the top of Gousta which
shone in the rays of the sun, while the Maan, bearing its
drifting logs, roared at his feet.

He could also see the people who passed on their road
from Dal to the Rjukanfos. Generally these were
tourists who stopped for an hour or two to lunch or dine at
the inn. Sometimes they were students from Christiania,
knapsack on back, with the Norwegian cockade in their
hats.

These recognized the professor. Hence cordial
greetings interminable, showing how popular Sylvius
Hog was with the young people.

"You here, Mr. Hog!"

"Yes, I am here, my friends."

"People thought you were in the depths of Hardanger."

"People thought wrong, then. I might have been in the depths of the Rjukanfos."

"Well, we'll tell everybody you are at Dal."

"Yes, at Dal, with a leg in a sling."

"Luckily you have fallen into good hands at Dame Hansen's inn."

"Can you imagine a better ? "

"Hardly."

"And better people ? "

"Not at all."

And then they all had a drink to the health of Hulda and Joel who were well known throughout Tellemarken.

And then the professor would tell his adventure. He would confess his imprudence and relate how he had been saved, and how some recognition was due to his rescuers.

"And if I stay here till I have paid my debt," he would add, "my course is finished for some time, my friends, and you can take an unlimited holiday."

"Ah, Mr. Sylvius," the group would reply, "it is the bewitching Hulda that keeps you at Dal."

"A nice girl, my friends, and a charming one, and I am only sixty, by Saint Olaf ! "

"Here's to your health, Mr. Sylvius."

"And to yours, my friends ! Tramp the country, teach yourselves, amuse yourselves. It is always fine weather at your age ; but beware the Maristien ! Joel and Hulda may not be there to pull out those who risk their lives there."

And then the students would hurry off, making the valley resound with their joyous " *God aften.*"

Once or twice Joel had to go away as guide to such tourists as wished to ascend Gousta. Sylvius Hog would have gone with him. He pretended he was cured, and, in fact, the graze on his leg had begun to heal over ; but Hulda positively forbade his exposing himself to fatigue that would be too great for him, and when Hulda gave orders he obeyed.

A curious mountain is this Gousta, whose central cone is furrowed with snow-filled ravines rising from a forest of firs like a green collar opening wide at its base. And what a circuit of view at its summit ! In the east the bailiwick of Numedal, in the west all Hardanger and its mighty glaciers ; then at the foot of the mountain the winding valley of Vestfjorddal, between lakes Mjos and Tinn, Dal and its houses in miniature, seemingly a box of children's toys, and the course of the Maan a luminous ribbon glittering as it winds through the verdure of the plains.

To make the ascent, Joel used to start at five o'clock in the morning and return at six o'clock in the afternoon. Sylvius Hog and Hulda went to meet him, waiting for him at the ferryman's hut. As soon as the ferry-boat had unloaded its passengers and their guide, there would be cordial handshakings; and a happy evening the three would spend together. The professor's leg still inconvenienced him a little, but he did not complain. It might indeed be said that he was in no hurry to get well, or rather to leave Dame Hansen's hospitable house.

But the time nevertheless passed rapidly. Sylvius Hog had written to Christiania that he would stay some

time at Dal. The report of his adventure at the Rjukanfos had spread all through the country. The papers
had described it. Some of them had put it into dramatic
form in their usual way. Hence a number of letters
arrived at the hostelry, besides pamphlets and newspapers. All these had to be read ; all these had to be
answered. Sylvius Hog read them and answered them,
and the names of Hulda and Joel occupied a place in
the correspondence, and travelled all over Norway.

But the stay with the Hansens could not be prolonged
indefinitely, and Sylvius Hog was no more decided than
at his arrival as to the way in which he could pay his
debt. He had begun to suspect that the family was not
so completely happy as he had thought. The impatience
with which brother and sister each day awaited the
postman from Christiania or Bergen, their disappointment, their dismay when they never had a letter, all this
was significant.

It was now the 9th of June, and no news of the *Viking !*
A delay of more than two weeks after the time fixed
for the return. Not a letter from Ole! Nothing to
soothe the torments of Hulda ! The poor girl was in
despair, and Sylvius Hog often saw that her eyes were
red when he first met her in the morning.

"What is the matter ?" he asked himself. "There
must be some sorrow they fear and hide from me. Is it a
family secret in which a stranger cannot share ? But am
I a stranger to them ? No ! they must not think that !
Perhaps when I tell them I am going away, they
may understand that it is a true friend who is leaving
them."

And that day he said to them,—

"My friends, the time is coming when to my great regret I shall have to leave you."

"Already, sir, already!" said Joel, with a vivacity he could not suppress.

"Eh! the time has gone quickly with you! It is seventeen days since I came to Dal."

"What! Seventeen days!"

"Yes, my dear girl, and my holiday is coming to an end! I have not a week to lose if I am to finish my trip to Drammen and Kongsberg. But it is to you that the Storthing is indebted for not having to fill up my seat, and the Storthing better than I will know how to reward you—"

"Oh, Mr. Sylvius!" interrupted Hulda, holding up her little hand and pretending to shut his mouth.

"That is so, Hulda! I am forbidden to say anything about it, and I must obey. But Joel and you will come and see me at Christiania?"

"See you, Mr. Sylvius?"

"Yes, see me—pass a few days in my house—with Dame Hansen, of course."

"And if we leave the inn, who is to look after it while we are away?" asked Joel.

"But the inn does not want you, I suppose, when the tourist season is over? And I intend to come and fetch you at the end of the autumn."

"Mr. Sylvius," said Hulda, "that will be very difficult."

"It will be very easy, on the contrary, my friends. Do not answer me. No! I will take no reply. And then, when I have got you in the best room of my house between my old Kate and my old Fink, you will be like my children, and you will have to tell me what I am to do for you."

"Do for us, Mr. Sylvius—" said Joel, looking at Hulda.

"Brother!" said Hulda, who understood what Joel was thinking of.

"Speak out, my boy, speak out!"

"Well, Mr. Sylvius, you can do us a very great honour."

"What?"

"If it does not inconvenience you too much you can come to my sister's wedding."

"Her wedding!" exclaimed Sylvius Hog; "what! my little Hulda going to get married! and she never yet told me a word about it!"

"Oh! Mr. Sylvius!" said the girl, her eyes filling with tears.

"And when is this wedding to be?"

"When it pleases God to bring back her betrothed to us."

CHAPTER XI.

THEN Joel told him all the history of Ole Kamp. He was much affected at the recital, and listened with profound attention. Now he knew all. He had just had read to him the last letter announcing Ole's return, and Ole had not returned. What anxiety, what misery for the Hansens!

"And I, who thought them all so happy!" thought he. And as he thought over the matter it seemed as though brother and sister would become desperate unless they were kept in hope. By keeping count of the days in May and June their imagination exaggerated the number as if they had counted them twice over.

The professor, therefore, gave his reasons—not convincing ones—but serious and plausible reasons why the *Viking* might have been delayed.

And as he did so a sorrowful look came over his face, for the dismay of Joel and Hulda had made a deep impression on him.

"Listen to me, my friends," he said, "sit down by my side and let us talk about this."

"And what can you tell us?" answered Hulda, her grief overcoming her.

"I will tell you what I think is right," said the professor, "and that is this. I have been thinking over what Joel has told me, and it seems to me that your anxiety is unreasonable. I would not give you illusory assurances, but it is well to look at things as they really are."

"Alas, Mr. Sylvius," said Hulda, "my poor Ole's lost with the *Viking*, and I shall never see him again."

"Sister! sister!" said Joel, "be calm, I pray you. Let us hear what Mr. Sylvius—"

"Keep calm, my children! See here! It was from the 15th to the 20th of May that Ole was to reach Bergen?"

"Yes," said Joel, "from the 15th to the 20th of May, as the letter said, and we are now at the 9th of June."

"That makes twenty days overdue since the extreme date given for the *Viking's* return. That is something we must admit. But a sailing vessel is not like a steam-ship."

"That is what I have been telling Hulda," said Joel, "and that is what I tell her now."

"And you have done well, my boy," said Sylvius Hog. "Besides the *Viking* may be an old boat, getting along but slowly like most of the Newfoundland vessels, especially if heavily laden. And there has been very rough weather during the last few weeks. And perhaps Ole did not put to sea as soon as he expected. In that case, it would only be eight days that the *Viking* is overdue, and that you have not received a letter from him. And do you know if the *Viking's* instructions did not leave her a certain latitude as to the choice of the port to which she could take her cargo in accordance with the state of the market?"

"Ole would have written," answered Hulda, who saw no hope to cling to.

"Who can prove he has not written?" answered the

professor. " And if he has, it is not the *Viking* that is overdue, but the mail from America. Suppose Ole's ship had to put in at one of the ports in the United States, that would explain why it is that his letters have not yet arrived in Europe—"

" In the United States, Mr. Sylvius ? "

" That happens sometimes, and you have only to miss the mail, to leave your friends without news for many days. Anyhow there is one very simple thing we can do, and that is to make inquiries of the owners at Bergen. Do you know them ? "

" Yes," said Joel, " Help Brothers."

" Help Brothers ! " exclaimed Sylvius Hog.

" Yes."

" And I know them too. The youngest, Help junior as they call him, is about my own age and one of my best friends ; we have often dined together at Christiania ! Help Brothers, my children ! Ah ! I shall learn all about the *Viking* from them. I'll write to them to-day, and if necessary, I'll go and see them."

" How good you are, Mr. Sylvius ! " said Hulda and Joel together.

" Oh, no thanks if you please ! I object to it ! Was I only to thank you for what you did over there? Now I get a chance of doing you a little service, and you are off at once."

" But you spoke of going to Christiania," said Joel.

" Well, I'll go to Bergen if it is necessary for me to go to Bergen."

" But then you will leave us, Mr. Sylvius," said Hulda.

" Well, then, I will not leave you, my dear girl ! I

am free to do as I like, I suppose, and until I have cleared up this matter, at least unless you show me the door—"

"What is that?"

"I have a good mind to stay at Dal till he comes back! I should like to know this sweetheart of my little Hulda! He ought to be a brave fellow—of the same sort as Joel!"

"Yes, he is just like him!" answered Hulda.

"I was sure of it," exclaimed the professor, whose good humour had returned to him—designedly probably.

"Ole is like Ole! Mr. Sylvius," said the brother, "and that means he is a really good fellow."

"Perhaps so, my gallant Joel, and that makes me all the more wish to see him. Something tells me that the *Viking* will soon return."

"Heaven hear you!"

"Why not? Yes. I will be at Hulda's wedding now you have asked me. The Storthing will have to extend my holiday for a week or so. It would have had to extend it considerably more if you had let me fall over the Rjukanfos as I deserved."

"Mr. Sylvius," said Joel, "it is very good of you to talk like that, and you have done a great deal for us—"

"Not as much as I could wish, my friends, for I owe you everything, and I know—"

"No! Say no more about it."

"On the contrary, I will say something more about it. Was it not I whom you seized from the claws of the Maristien? Was it not I whom you risked your life to save? Was it not I whom you brought to this inn at Dal? Was it not I whom you took care of and cured without any help from the doctors ? But I am as obstinate as a carriole horse, I warn you ; and I have taken it into my head to be present at the wedding of Hulda and Ole Kamp, and by Saint Olaf, I shall be present ! "

Confidence is communicative. How was it possible to resist such confidence as that shown by Sylvius Hog? He saw that a half smile lighted up poor Hulda's face. She wanted but to believe—she wanted but to hope.

Sylvius Hog then continued,—

" But we must remember that time is going quickly. We must begin our preparations for the wedding ! "

" We have begun them, Mr. Sylvius," said Hulda, " and we began them three weeks ago."

" Capital ! Well, we must take care and not interrupt them."

" Interrupt them ? " answered Joel. " But everything is ready."

" What ! the bride's skirt, the bodice with the filagree clasps, the belt, and the pendants ! "

" Even the pendants ! "

" And the radiant coronet which will crown you as if you were a saint, my little Hulda ? "

" Yes, Mr. Sylvius."

" And the invitations are out ? "

" All of them, even the one we think most of, and that is yours."

" And the bridesmaid has been chosen from among the wisest girls in Tellemarken ? "

" And the prettiest, Mr. Sylvius," said Joel, "for she is Siegfrid Helmboë of Bamble !

"With what an air he said that!" said the professor. "And how he blushed as he said it! Eh! Eh! And by any chance is Mademoiselle Siegfrid Helmboë of Bamble destined to become Madame Joel Hansen of Dal?"

"Yes, Mr. Sylvius," answered Hulda, "Siegfrid is my greatest friend."

"Good! another wedding!" exclaimed Sylvius Hog, "and I am sure I shall be asked, and I cannot do otherwise than accept. I had better send in my resignation to the Storthing for I shall have no time to sit! Well, I will be your witness, Joel, after having first been your sister's, if you will allow me! Kiss me, Hulda! Shake hands, my lad! and now be off while I write to my friend Help junior, of Bergen!"

The brother and sister left the ground-floor room which the professor talked about taking on a lease, and returned to their work in a little more hopeful mood.

Sylvius Hog remained alone.

"Poor girl! poor girl!" he said to himself. "Yes! I have for a moment outgeneraled her grief! I have given her a little calm! But it is a long delay, and in such stormy seas as now! If the *Viking* has gone down! If Ole never comes back!"

A minute afterwards the professor was writing to the owners at Bergen. He asked in his letter for precise details as to all that concerned the *Viking* and her fishing campaign. He wished to know if any circumstances, foreseen or otherwise, had obliged her to change her port of destination. It was important for him to know as soon as possible what the merchants and sailors of Bergen thought of the delay. Finally he begged his friend, Help junior, to ascertain all he could and let him know by return of post.

This pressing letter also said why Sylvius Hog was so much interested in the young captain of the *Viking*. For what service he was indebted to his sweetheart, and what happiness it would be to him to give any happiness to the children of Dame Hansen.

As soon as the letter was written Joel took it to the post at Mœl. It would go out next day. On the 11th of June it would be at Bergen : on the 12th in the evening or on the 13th in the morning, at the latest, Mr. Help junior would reply.

Nearly three days to wait ! How long they seemed ! By reassuring words and encouraging reasons the professor did what he could to make the waiting less trying. Now that he knew Hulda's secret, was not the subject of conversation marked out for him ? And what consolation for Joel and his sister could be better than speaking constantly of the absent one ?

" Now, am I not one of your family ? " asked Sylvius Hog. " Yes, a sort of an uncle come home from America —or somewhere else ? "

And as he was one of the family, there could be no secrets from him. He had never failed to remark the attitude of the two children towards their mother. The reserve Dame Hansen affected to maintain seemed to him to have another cause than the non-arrival of Ole Kamp. He spoke about it to Joel. Joel did not know what to say. He would then have liked to ask Dame Hansen, but the dame kept herself so close that he did not like to pry into her secrets. The future would reveal all without doubt.

G 2

As Sylvius Hog expected, Help junior's reply arrived at Dal on the morning of the 13th. Joel had been waiting for the postman since daybreak, and he it was who brought in the letter to the professor, who was sitting with Dame Hansen and her daughter.

There was a moment of silence. Hulda turned pale, and could not speak for the violent beating of her heart. She clasped the hand of her brother, and he was as much affected as she was.

Sylvius Hog opened the letter and read it aloud.

To his great regret Help junior's reply contained only vague indications, and the professor could not hide his disappointment from the young people, who listened to him with tears in their eyes.

The *Viking* had left St. Pierre Miquelon on the date stated in Ole's last letter. That they had ascertained from other ships which had arrived at Bergen, having left after the *Viking*. These ships had not spoken her on the passage. But they had made very bad weather of it round the islands. They had come through, but perhaps the *Viking* had not done so well, and had put back to one of the ports in the island. She was a good ship and very strong, and had an excellent crew; but the delay was disquieting, and if it lasted much longer there would be reason to believe that the *Viking* had gone down with all on board.

Help junior regretted to have no better news of the young relative of the Hansens. He could speak most favourably of Ole Kamp, and he was well worthy of all the sympathy felt for him by Sylvius Hog.

Help junior finished by assuring the professor of his

friendship and sending his regards to the family ; and he promised to let him know as soon as possible if anything was heard concerning the *Viking* from any Norwegian port, and he begged to remain, very faithfully yours, Help Brothers.

Poor Hulda almost fainted in the chair as Sylvius read the letter, and burst into sobs when he had finished.

Joel, with arms crossed, heard and said nothing, without even daring to look at his sister.

Dame Hansen, when Sylvius had ceased reading, rose and retired to her room. It seemed as though she had expected this misfortune, as she had expected others.

The professor beckoned to Hulda and her brother to come near him. He wished to speak to them about Ole Kamp, to tell them all that his imagination suggested more or less possible with regard to the delay, and he expressed himself with strange assurance even after the receipt of such a letter. He had a presentiment ! He in no way despaired ! Was there not many an example of long delays in crossing the seas between Norway and Newfoundland ? Yes ; undoubtedly. The *Viking* was a strong ship, well commanded, with an excellent crew, and consequently in better condition than those that had come into port.

"Let us hope, then, my children, and wait ! If the *Viking* had been wrecked between Iceland and Newfoundland, would not the numerous ships on that route to Europe have come across some traces of the wreck ? Well, not a fragment had been seen in a neighbourhood so frequented by vessels returning from the fishery ! Nevertheless, something must be done, more certain news must be obtained. If after this week we are still without news of the *Viking*, and have no letter from Ole, I will return to Christiania, I will address myself to the Shipping Board, who will take the matter up, and, I am convinced, to the satisfaction of us all."

Whatever confidence the professor showed, Joel and Hulda felt clearly enough that he did not speak now as he did before he received Help's letter—a letter which left little room for hope. Sylvius never now alluded to the approaching marriage of Hulda and Ole Kamp, although all the time he kept saying to himself,—

"No! it is not possible! For Ole never again to enter this house! for Ole not to marry Hulda! Never will I believe such a calamity to be possible!"

This was his own conviction. He felt it with all the energy of his character which nothing could withstand. But how could he share it with others, and above all with those whom the fate of the *Viking* affected so intimately?

A few days went by. Sylvius Hog, completely restored to health, took long walks in the neighbourhood. He obliged Hulda and her brother to accompany him, so as not to leave them alone. One day they went up the valley of Vestfjorddal, halfway to the Rjukanfos; the next they went down it towards Mœl and Lake Tinn. Once even they were absent for four-and-twenty hours. This was when they prolonged their excursion to Bamble, where the professor made acquaintance with farmer Helmboë and his daughter Siegfrid. Kind was the reception which Siegfrid gave her friend, and tender was the sympathy with which she consoled her.

Again Sylvius Hog inspired a little hope in his friends. He had written to the Shipping Board at

Christiania.   The Government were inquiring about the
Viking.   They would find her out.   Ole would come
back.   He might be back any day.   No! the wedding
would not be six weeks late! The excellent man
seemed so convinced himself, that they were moved
perhaps more by this conviction than by his arguments.

The visit to the Helmboës did the Hansens some
good, and when they returned home they were much
more resigned than when they had set out.

It was now the 15th of June.   The *Viking* was a
month overdue.   For the short passage between Newfoundland and Norway this was certainly excessive—
even for a sailing vessel.

Hulda was hardly living.   Her brother could not find
a consoling word to say to her ; and the professor suc-
cumbed in the task he had set himself of breathing hope
into them.   Hulda and Joel only left the house to look
down the Mœl road or up the way to the Rjukanfos.
Ole Kamp might come by Bergen, but he might come
by Christiania if his destination had been altered.   The
rumble of an approaching carriole heard under the trees,
a shout in the distance, the figure of a man turning the
corner of the road, would make their hearts beat, but all
was in vain !   The people of Dal watched on their part.
They met the postman up and down the Maan ; everybody interested himself in the family that was so much
liked in the country, in this poor Ole who was almost a
child of Tellemarken ; and not a letter came from Bergen
or Christiania bringing news of the absent.

On the 16th nothing new happened.   Sylvius Hog
could not remain any longer where he was.   He saw he
must do something himself, and so he gave out that on the

morrow if nothing arrived he would be off to Christiania, and assure himself that something was being done. He did not like leaving Hulda and Joel, but he must do so, and he would return as soon as he had finished his business.

On the 17th the greater part of the day had gone, the saddest of all, perhaps. The rain had not ceased to fall since the morning. The wind tore through the trees, and swept the torrent like hail against the windows.

It was seven o'clock. They had finished dinner in silence as if it were a house of mourning. Sylvius Hog had not even been able to keep up the conversation. Words and ideas failed him. What could he say that he had not said a hundred times already?

"I will start to-morrow for Christiania," said he. "Joel, see about getting a carriole. You can take me to Mœl, and return at once to Dal."

"Yes, Mr. Sylvius," said Joel. "You do not wish me to go further with you?"

The professor shook his head and pointed to Hulda, who would not have liked to be parted from her brother.

At this moment there was a noise just audible along the road from Mœl. All listened. Soon there could be no doubt. It was the sound of a carriole coming rapidly towards Dal. Was it some traveller going to pass the night at the inn? That was not likely, as tourists very rarely arrived so late.

Hulda stood up trembling all over. Joel went to the door, opened it, and looked out.

The noise increased. It was certainly the trotting of a horse and the rumble of carriole wheels. But such was the fury of the storm that the door had to be shut.

Sylvius Hog strode up and down the room. Joel and his sister kept close to each other.

The carriole could not be twenty yards from the house. Was it going to stop or pass by?

Their hearts beat—horribly.

The carriole stopped. They heard a voice calling. It was not the voice of Ole Kamp!

Almost immediately there came a knock at the door.

Joel opened it.

A man was on the threshold.

"Mr. Sylvius Hog?" he asked.

"I am he," answered the professor as he came forward.

"Who are you, my friend?"

"An express sent to you from Christiania by the secretary of the Shipping Board."

"You have a letter for me?"

"It is here!"

And the express presented a large envelope fastened with an official seal.

Hulda had not strength to remain standing. Her brother had just sat her down in the chair. Neither of them dare hurry the professor to open the letter.

At last he read as follows :—

"In reply to your last letter, I herewith enclose you a document which was found at sea by a Danish ship, on the 3rd of June last. Unfortunately this document leaves no doubt as to the fate of the *Viking*—"

Sylvius Hog, without stopping to finish the letter, drew the document from the envelope. He looked at it —he turned it over.

It was a lottery ticket bearing the number 9672. At the back of the ticket were these few lines :—

" 3rd May.—Dear Hulda, the *Viking* is going down. This ticket is all I possess. I trust it to God for Him to bring it to you, and if I am not there, I beg you will be there when it is drawn. My last thoughts are for you. Hulda, don't forget me in your prayers ! Good-bye, my own, good-bye.

" OLE KAMP."

It was a lottery ticket.

CHAPTER XII.

THIS, then, was the young sailor's secret. This was the chance on which he reckoned to win a fortune for his betrothed. A lottery ticket bought before he left! And at the moment when the *Viking* was sinking he had put it into a bottle and thrown it into the sea with a last good-bye to Hulda!

This time Sylvius Hog was annihilated. He looked at the letter, then at the document! He said nothing. What could he say? What doubt could there now be as to the loss of the *Viking* and all on board?

Hulda, while Sylvius Hog read the letter, bore up against the anguish, but as the last words were uttered she fell back senseless in Joel's arms, and was carried off to her room, where her mother looked after her.

When Dame Hansen returned, she stepped up towards the professor as though she would have spoken to him, and then going towards the staircase she disappeared.

Joel, after leaving his sister, also went out. He was being suffocated in the house which was open to all the winds of misfortune. He must have some fresh air, the air of the storm, and for a part of the night he remained wandering on the banks of the Maan.

Sylvius Hog was left alone. At first he was thunder-struck, but he soon recovered his habitual energy.

After taking two or three turns of the room, he stopped and listened in case a cry from the girl should reach him; and then he sat down at the table and gave himself over to his reflections.

"For Hulda," he said, "never again to see her betrothed! It cannot be! No! My whole being revolts from the very thought! The *Viking* may have foundered! But that is no certain proof of Ole's death! I cannot believe it! In all these cases of shipwreck it is only time alone that can say that no one has survived the catastrophe. Yes! I doubt and I will doubt, though neither Hulda, nor Joel, nor anybody else will share the doubt with me. If the *Viking* foundered, that explains why there was no wreckage, nothing but this bottle in which poor Ole put his last thought, and with it all he had in the world."

Sylvius Hog held in his hand the document. He looked at it, he shook it, he turned it over; this scrap of paper on which the poor boy had built all his hopes of fortune. Then the professor, wishing to examine it more carefully, rose from his chair, listened if the poor girl was calling for her mother or brother, and crossed into his room.

The ticket was the ticket of a lottery of the Christiania Schools, then a very popular lottery in Norway. First prize a hundred thousand marks, total value of the other prizes, ninety thousand marks. Number of tickets issued, a million—none being blanks.

The ticket bore the number 9672. But whether this number was good or bad, or the young sailor had or had not any secret reasons for his confidence, would not be known till the drawing which was fixed for the ensuing

15th July, that is to say, in twenty-eight days more. Hulda according to his last injunctions would represent him, and she would answer for him.

Sylvius Hog by the light of his candle re-read the lines on the back of the ticket, as if he would discover some hidden sense in them.

The lines had been written in ink. They showed that Ole's hand had not trembled while he wrote them. That proved that the master of the *Viking* had not lost his self-command when the wreck took place. He was thus in a position to avail himself of any means of safety that might offer itself, any spar or plank, if everything had not been swallowed by the waves.

Generally these documents saved from the sea give a clue as to the position in which the catastrophe occurred. But here there was neither latitude nor longitude, nothing to indicate the writer was near land, either continent or islands. It was to be concluded then that neither the captain nor crew of the *Viking* knew where they were. Seized doubtless by one of those tempests which there is no resisting they had been driven out of their course, and the state of the weather had prevented their taking a solar observation, so that their position had not been fixed for some days. It was then probable that they did not know whereabouts in the north Atlantic, off Newfoundland or Iceland, they had been driven by the storm.

Herein lày a circumstance which would give à little hope to those who would not despair. In fact with such vague indications researches could be undertaken, and a ship could be sent to the scene of the catastrophe to pick up a few of the recognizable remains. Who

knew whether a few of the survivors of the crew might
not have reached some point on the Arctic continent
where they were now without help, and without means
of getting home ?   Such was the doubt which gradually
took possession of Sylvius Hog—a doubt which neither
Hulda nor Joel could entertain, a doubt which the professor hesitated to suggest to them.

" Besides," said he to himself, "if the document gives no
indication we can make use of, they at least know where
the bottle was picked up !   This letter does not say
so, but the Shipping Board at Christiania could not be
ignorant of it.   That is something we might profit by.
In working out the direction of the currents, and of the
wind in connection with the assumed date of the wreck,
we might do something.   I'll write again.   It is necessary that I should urge them on if no chance is to escape
us.   No !   I will never abandon my poor Hulda !   Never
without absolute proof will I believe her lover to be dead."

Thus reasoned Sylvius Hog.   But at the same time
he took care to say nothing about the steps he was
going to take, or the efforts he was about to use his
influence to urge on.   Neither Hulda nor her brother
knew that he had written to Christiania.   On the other
hand, the departure he had spoken of taking next day,
he had resolved to postpone indefinitely—or rather he
would start in a few days for Bergen.   Then he would
learn from Messrs. Help all that concerned the *Viking*,
he would take the advice of the most competent seamen,
and would decide on the manner in which he should set
about his search.

Meanwhile, on information furnished by the Shipping
Board, the newspapers of Christiania, and then those of

Norway and Sweden, and then those of Europe, had
gradually published the facts about the lottery ticket.
There was something touching in this message from a
sailor to his betrothed, and public opinion was interested
in it, and not unreasonably.

The chief of the Norwegian journals, the *Morgenblad*,
was the first to report the incident of the *Viking* and
Ole Kamp. Of the thirty-seven other newspapers then
appearing in the country not one omitted to say something about it in appreciative terms. The *Illustreret
Nyhedsblad* published an ideal design of the scene of the
wreck. The *Viking* was seen disappearing beneath the
waves, with her sails in ribbons and her masts half
carried away, while Ole, standing in the bow was
throwing his bottle into the sea as he gave his last
thought to Hulda and his soul to God. In allegorical
distance there was a light cloud, and in the cloud was
a wave bringing the bottle to the feet of his betrothed.
The whole was enclosed in the frame of the lottery
ticket with the number fully displayed. A childish
design, no doubt, but one that would have great success
in countries still attached to the legends of the Undines
and the Valkyries.

Then the news was reproduced and commented on
in England, France, and even in the United States of
America. The story of Hulda and Ole was popularized
by the pencil and the pen. The young Norwegian of
Dal, without knowing it, had been privileged to interest
public opinion, and could hardly believe in the noise
that was made about her, though nothing could draw
her thoughts away from the grief which mastered her.

And we need not be astonished at another effect

produced in both continents—an effect easily intelligible
when we remember how easily human nature sinks into
superstition. A lottery ticket recovered under such
circumstances, with this number 9672, so providentially
rescued from the waves, could not be other than a fateful
ticket. Was it not miraculously predestined to carry
off the big prize of 100,000 marks ? Was it not worth
a fortune—the fortune on which Ole Kamp had
reckoned ?

And so it is not to be wondered at that there came to
Dal very serious propositions for the purchase of this
ticket should Hulda Hansen care to sell it. At first
the prices offered were mediocre, but they rose from day
to day. As the day approached for the drawing, the
bidding became quite serious.

These offers came not only from Scandinavian
countries, so ready to recognize the intervention of supernatural powers in the things of this world, but from
foreign countries, and even from France. The English
phlegmatically joined in, and after them came the Ameri-
cans, whose dollars are never very cheerfully parted with
in such unpractical speculations. The letters came to
Dal, and the newspapers did not fail to keep the public
informed of the offers made to the Hansens. It might
almost be said that a small stock exchange was started
in which the prices were always shifting, but always with
a tendency upwards.

And in fact many hundreds of marks were offered for
the ticket which only stood a millionth chance in the
draw. This was absurd without doubt, but there is no
reason in superstitious notions. And so the fancy grew,
and with the acquired force the offers grew. Eight days

after the original announcement the newspapers informed
their readers that the offers had exceeded a thousand,
fifteen hundred, and even two thousand marks. An
Englishman at Manchester had even offered £100 or
about 2500 marks. An American at Boston improved
on this, and proposed to purchase ticket No. 9672 for
the sum of 1000 dollars or about 5000 marks.

It need not be said that Hulda took no interest in
what was so passionately exciting the public. With the
letters arriving at Dal about the ticket she had no wish
to be bothered. However, the professor thought she
ought not to remain ignorant of the proposals that
had been made, for Ole Kamp had assigned to her his
property in the ticket. Hulda refused all the offers.
The ticket was the last letter from her betrothed.

And it will not easily be believed that the poor girl
clung to it only with an idea to its value as one of the
chances in a lottery. No! She saw in it the last farewell of her shipwrecked lover, a last relic she would ever
treasure. She hardly thought of the fortune that Ole
could not share with her.

In keeping her aware of the offers made for it, neither
Sylvius Hog nor Joel intended to influence her. She
had only to trust to the promptings of her own heart,
and we know how her heart responded. And Joel
fully approved of his sister's decision. Ole Kamp's
letter ought to be given up to nobody—on no considera-
tion whatever.

Sylvius Hog also approved of Hulda's action, and
congratulated her on turning a deaf ear to this trading.
Were they to see this ticket sold to one, re-sold to
another, passing from hand to hand, transformed into a

sort of paper-money up to the time when the drawing took place, and then probably become a mere piece of waste paper?

And Sylvius Hog went further. Was he after all superstitious? No, certainly not. But if Ole Kamp had been there he would probably have said to him,—

"Keep your ticket, my boy, keep it! It has been saved from shipwreck, and so have you! Wait and see! We do not know. No one knows."

And when Sylvius Hog, professor of jurisprudence and member of the Storthing, thought like that, can we be astonished at the infatuation of the public?

No; and nothing could be more natural than that No. 9672 was at a premium.

In Dame Hansen's house there was nobody who objected to the girl's praiseworthy sentiment—except the dame herself.

Often would she be heard grumbling in Hulda's absence, and thus causing considerable pain to Joel. She would secretly talk to Hulda about the offers that were being made.

"Five thousand marks for that ticket!" she would say "They have offered five thousand marks!"

Evidently Dame Hansen saw nothing touching in her daughter's refusal. All she thought of was the important sum of five thousand marks. A word from Hulda would bring them into the house. She had no belief in the supernatural value of the ticket, Norwegian though she was. And to sacrifice five thousand marks for the millionth chance of winning a hundred thousand did not enter the thoughts of her cold, positive nature.

It was obvious that to reject the certain for the uncertain even under the contingent circumstances was not wise. But we repeat, the ticket was not a lottery ticket for Hulda, it was Ole Kamp's last letter, and her heart would have broken at the thought of having it taken away from her.

Nevertheless Dame Hansen manifestly disapproved of the conduct of her daughter, and was fostering a secret irritation against her. Any day it was to be feared she would attempt to make Hulda change her mind. Already she had spoken in this sense to Joel, and he had at once taken his sister's part.

Naturally Sylvius Hog was informed of what was taking place. It was one sorrow more for Hulda, and he regretted it.

Several times Joel asked him,—

"Is my sister right in refusing? Have I done well in approving of her refusal?"

"Certainly," answered the professor. "From a mathematical point of view your mother is right! But mathematics are not everything in this world! Arithmetic has nothing to do with the affairs of the heart."

For a fortnight Hulda had to be carefully watched. Overwhelmed by so much grief there were serious fears for her sanity. Fortunately she was well cared for. At the request of Sylvius Hog, his friend the famous Dr. Boek came to Dal to see the invalid. All he could prescribe was rest and quiet for the mind if that were possible. But the only cure was Ole's return, and this God alone could give. Sylvius Hog did all he could to console the poor girl, and never ceased from giving her words of hope. And although everything seemed improbable, yet Sylvius Hog did not despair.

Thirteen days had elapsed since the arrival of the letter sent by the Shipping Board to Dal. It was the 30th of June. Fifteen days, and the lottery would be drawn with great ceremony in one of the large halls of Christiania!

On the 30th of June, in the morning, Sylvius Hog received another letter from the maritime authorities at Bergen. They had arranged, with the consent of the Government, for an immediate search with regard to the *Viking*.

The professor said nothing to Joel or Hulda as to what was in progress. He contented himself with announcing his departure, and pretended that he must leave on business which would keep him away a few days.

"Mr. Sylvius," said Hulda, "I beseech you, do not leave us."

"Leave you—you who have become my children!" replied Sylvius Hog.

Joel offered to accompany him. But not wishing him to suspect he had gone to Bergen, he did not allow him to come farther than Mœl. Besides it would not do to leave Hulda alone with her mother. After keeping her bed for several days, she was now able to get up; but she was still weak, she remained in her room, and her brother felt that he ought not to leave her.

At eleven o'clock the carriole was at the inn-door; the professor took his place in it with Joel, after bidding a last farewell to Hulda. Then they disappeared at the turn in the road under the large birches by the river-bank.

That evening Joel was to return to Dal,

CHAPTER XIII.

SYLVIUS HOG had thus started for Bergen. His tena-
cious nature, his energetic character, for an instant
overwhelmed, had reasserted themselves. He would not
believe in Ole Kamp's death, nor admit that Hulda was
doomed to see him no more. No! The more unmistak-
able the facts the less he believed in them. As is
vulgarly said, "they were a little too strong for him."

Had he, then, any clue to which he could direct his
efforts at Bergen? Yes; but a very vague clue it must
be confessed.

He knew the date the ticket had been thrown into
the sea by Ole, and the date and position in which the
bottle containing it had been picked up. This is what
he had learnt from the Shipping Office in the letter which
decided him to go to Bergen, and consult with Messrs.
Help and the most competent seamen of the port.
Perhaps that would be enough to give a useful direction
to the search of which the *Viking* was to be the object.

The journey was accomplished as rapidly as possible.
Arrived at Mœl, Sylvius Hog sent back his companion
with the carriole. He took passage in one of the
birch-bark boats that ply on Lake Tinn, at Tinoset,
instead of starting southwards, that is to say towards
Bamble; he hired a second carriole, and took the road
to Hardanger, so as to gain the gulf of this name by

the shortest road. There the *Rime*, a little steamboat
which plies in the gulf, took him to its farthest end, and
then, after traversing a network of fjords among the
islands and isles with which the Norwegian coast is
crowded, on the 2nd of July, at dawn, he landed at
Bergen.

This ancient town, on the shores of the two fjords of
Sogno and Hardanger, is situated in a superb country
which will resemble Switzerland when an artificial arm
of the sea brings the waters of the Mediterranean to the
foot of the mountains. A magnificent avenue of ash
trees gives access to the chief houses of Bergen. Its high
buildings with pointed gables, resplendently white like
those in Arab towns, are crowded into an irregular tri-
angle containing 30,000 inhabitants. Its churches date
from the twelfth century. Its lofty cathedral forms a
conspicuous landmark for vessels in the offing. It is
the commercial capital of Norway, although situated
away from the lines of communication, and at a considerable distance from the two other towns which poli-
tically hold the first and second rank in the kingdom
—Christiania and Drontheim.

Under any other circumstances the professor would
have devoted much attention to this important town,
which is more Dutch than Norwegian in its aspect and
customs. That was in the original programme of his
journey. But since his adventure at the Maristien, and
his arrival at Dal, the programme had undergone important modifications. Sylvius Hog was no longer the
tourist member personally studying the country from a
political and commercial point of view. He was the
guest of the Hansen house, and under obligation to

Hulda and Joel whose interests dominated everything. He was the debtor, who at any price wished to pay his debt of gratitude, and, he thought to himself, what he was now doing for them would be very little after all!

On arriving at Bergen in the *Rime*, Sylvius Hog landed at the fish market; thence he went off to the Tyske-Bodrone quarter, where lived Help junior, of the house of Help Brothers. Naturally it was raining, for it rains at Bergen three hundred and sixty days in the year. But it would be difficult to find a better-managed house than that of Help junior. The professor had no cause to complain of his welcome, which was as warm, cordial, and demonstrative as he could wish. His friend possessed himself of him as if he were a precious stone which was to be stored with care, and only given up in exchange for a receipt in due and proper form.

Immediately Sylvius Hog acquainted Help junior with the object of his journey. He spoke about the *Viking*. He asked if any news had come since his last letter. Did the sailors in the place think her lost? Had not the wreck, which threw many people into mourning, caused the authorities to take any steps with regard to it?

"And how could they?" answered Help junior, "for we don't know where it took place."

"That, my dear Help, is precisely what they should find out."

"Find out?"

"Yes! If you know nothing about the place where the *Viking* went down, you at least know where the document was picked up by the Dane. That is a clue we should not neglect."

" Where was that ? "

" Listen, my dear Help."

And then Sylvius Hog related what he had last heard from the Shipping Office, and showed the full powers that had been given him to act.

The bottle which contained Ole Kamp's lottery ticket had been found on the 3rd of June by the brigantine *Christian*, Captain Mosselman, of Elsinore, two hundred miles south-west of Iceland, with the wind blowing from south-west. The captain had immediately taken note of the document, as he should have done, in case of a relief being attempted for the survivors of the *Viking*. But the lines written on the back of the ticket gave no indication of the place of the wreck, and the *Christian* could not bear up for the scene of the catastrophe.

An honest man was Captain Mosselman. Perhaps another, less scrupulous, would have kept the ticket for himself. He never had but one thought, and that was to send it at once to the address as soon as he came into port. Hulda Hansen of Dal that was enough. It was not necessary to know more.

But when he came ashore, it seemed to him it would be better to hand over the document to the Danish authorities instead of sending it direct. That would be safer and more regular. That, therefore, was what he did, and the Marine Office at Copenhagen had immediately informed the Shipping Board at Christiania.

At that time they had already received Sylvius Hog's first letters of inquiry about the *Viking*. The special interest he took in the Hansen family was known. Sylvius Hog was to be at Dal for some time as they knew, and so the document received from the Danish captain was sent on to him to hand over to Hulda Hansen.

Since then the story had not ceased to interest the public. Thanks to the touching details added by the newspapers, they had in no way forgotten it.

Such was what Sylvius Hog told his friend Help junior, who listened with great interest without interruption until he had finished the recital.

"There is one point of which there is no doubt, and that is that on the 3rd of June the document was found two hundred miles south-west of Iceland, a month after the *Viking* had sailed from St. Pierre Miquelon for Europe."

"And you know nothing else?''

"No, my dear Help, but by consulting the most experienced sailors who are practically acquainted with those parts, knowing the general direction of the winds, and particularly the currents, could we not make out the course taken by the bottle? And then, taking count of its speed and the time elapsed before it was recovered, would it not be possible to imagine whereabouts it was thrown overboard by Ole Kamp, in other words the scene of the shipwreck?"

Help junior shook his head doubtfully. To base the search on such vague indications, in which were so many chances of error, was to run almost certain risk of failure. The owner was of a cool, practical nature, and considered it right to tell the professor this.

"Quite so, friend Help! But if we can only obtain very uncertain data that is no reason for our giving up the game. We ought to try everything for the sake of these poor people to whom I owe my life, and,

if necessary, I shall not hesitate to sacrifice all I have
got to find Ole Kamp and restore him to his betrothed,
Hulda Hansen."

And then Sylvius Hog related in detail his adventure
at the Rjukanfos. He told him how the intrepid Joel
and his sister had risked their lives to save him, and
how without their intervention he would not have had
the pleasure of then paying his respects to his friend
Help.

Friend Help, as we have said, was little inclined to
pay attention to illusions ; but he was not opposed to
what might be useless or even impossible if it was a
question of humanity. So he finally approved of what
the professor proposed to attempt.

" Sylvius," he said, " I will assist you as much as I
can. Yes ! You are right ! Although there is but a
very slight chance of finding any survivor of the *Viking*,
and among the rest this man Kamp, whose betrothed
saved your life, yet we must not miss it."

" No, Help, no ! Not if there be but one chance in a
hundred thousand."

" This very day I will invite all the best seamen in
Bergen to come to my office. I will appeal to all who
have cruised about the neighbourhood of Iceland and
Newfoundland. And we will see what they advise us
to do—"

" And what they advise us to do, we will do ! " said
the professor with his usual ardour. " I have the support of the Government. I am authorized to send off
one of the despatch boats in search of the *Viking*, and I
don't think any one should hesitate to help in such a
work."

"I will go to the Shipping Office," said Help junior.

"Would you like me to go with you?"

"It would be useless! You are tired!"

"Tired! and at my age!"

"Does not matter! Rest yourself, my dear and always youthful Sylvius, and wait for me here."

That very day there was a meeting of captains of merchantmen, fishing-boats, and pilots at the office of Help Brothers. Among them were many who were still at work and many who had retired.

At the outset Sylvius Hog told them how matters stood. He told them at what date—3rd May—the document had been thrown into the water by Ole Kamp, at what date—3rd June—the Danish captain had found it, and in what position, two hundred miles south-west of Iceland.

The discussion was long and serious. There was not one of these men who did not know the neighbourhood of Iceland and the Newfoundland seas, and the general direction of the currents which it was necessary to take into account to solve the problem.

It was certain that at the time of the wreck, during the interval comprised between the departure of the *Viking* from St. Pierre Miquelon and the recovery of the bottle by the Danish ship, incessant squalls from the south-west had swept across this part of the Atlantic. To these storms the catastrophe was doubtless due. Probably the *Viking*, finding it impossible to lay to, had had to run before the wind. This was during the equinox, at the time the polar ice begins to appear in the Atlantic.   It was thus possible that a collision had taken place, and that the *Viking* had been crushed by one of these moving reefs which it is so difficult to avoid.

If this were so, why should not the crew, or a portion of it, be taking refuge on one of the ice fields with a certain quantity of provisions! If that were so, the mass of ice would be driven back to the north-west, and it was not impossible that the survivors had at length reached land somewhere on the Greenland coast. It was, thus, in that direction that the survivors should be looked for.

Such was the verdict of this meeting of ancient mariners. There could be no doubt the attempt ought to be made as indicated. But what was to be done if there was no wreckage, in the case of the *Viking* having been sunk by an iceberg? Could they reckon on the return of the survivors of the wreck? A very dubious affair this! The professor saw that the most competent men could not or would not answer. That was no reason for doing nothing, for on the other matter they were agreed.

Bergen has always a few ships of the Norwegian navy in its harbour. At the port there is stationed one of the three despatch boats working between Drontheim, Finmark, Hammerfest, and the North Cape. At this time one of these despatch boats was at anchor in the bay.

After drawing up a note giving the opinions of the sailors called together by Help junior, Sylvius Hog went on board the *Telegraf*, and there informed the commander of the special mission he had been entrusted with by the Government.

The commander received the professor with cordiality, and declared himself ready to assist him in every possible way. He had already traversed these seas during the long perilous seasons of the Bergen fishermen off the banks, and could bring his personal knowledge to bear in the work of humanity.

As for the memorandum handed him by Sylvius Hog indicating the presumed place of the wreck, he quite approved of its conclusions. It was in that part of the sea between Iceland and Greenland that the survivors or traces of the *Viking* should be looked for. If the commander did not succeed there, he would explore the adjoining districts and Baffin's Bay on the eastern side.

"I am ready to start," said he, "my coals and stores are all on board, and I can be off this very day."

"Thank you, captain," said the professor, "I am much touched by the welcome you have given me. But one more question. Can you tell me how long it will take you to reach Greenland?"

"My boat goes nine knots an hour. And as the distance from Bergen to Greenland is about twenty degrees, I think we ought to be there in eight days."

"Make all the speed you can, then," said Sylvius. "If any of the men have survived the wreck, they will have been two months in a state of destitution, and doubtless dying with hunger on some desert coast—"

"There is not any time to lose. I shall sail to-day with the ebb, and keep up full speed; and as soon as I have found any clue I will send on to Christiania by the Newfoundland cable."

"Go then, captain, and success be yours!"

That very day the *Telegraf* prepared for the voyage, greeted by the sympathetic hurrahs of the whole population of Bergen. And it was not without much emotion that she steamed down the passes and disappeared behind the last islet in the fjord.

But Sylvius Hog did not slacken in his efforts with this expedition on which he had sent the *Telegraf*. In his estimation more was to be done in multiplying the means of finding some trace of the *Viking*. Was it not possible to excite some emulation among the merchant and fishing vessels, and to give some plan to their searches as they sailed between Iceland and the Faroes? Yes, certainly. And so he offered a prize of two thousand marks in the name of the State for any vessel that would furnish a clue to the lost ship, and five thousand marks for any vessel that would bring off any of the survivors of the wreck.

In the two days he passed at Bergen, Sylvius had done all that was possible to insure the success of his campaign. He had been ably seconded by his great friend Help junior and the maritime authorities. Help wished him to stay for some time with him. The professor thanked him, and refused to prolong his visit. He was anxious to rejoin Hulda and Joel, whom he feared to leave too long by themselves. But Help junior agreed with him that if any news arrived it could be sent on immediately to Dal. To him alone belonged the task of informing the Hansens.

On the morning of the 4th, Sylvius Hog said farewell to his friend Help junior, and re-embarked on the *Rime* for the voyage down Hardanger fjord. And, unless some unlikely delay took place, he reckoned on reaching Tellemarken on the evening of the 5th.

CHAPTER XIV.

THE day Sylvius Hog left Bremen, there was an important scene at the inn at Dal.

After the professor's departure it seemed as though the inn was empty. It seemed as though the good genius of Hulda and Joel had taken away, with their last hope, all the life of the family. It was as it were a house of the dead that he left behind him.

During these days no tourists came to Dal. Joel had no need to be away, and he was able to remain with Hulda, whom he was very anxious not to leave by herself.

Dame Hansen suffered more and more from her secret anxiety. She seemed to be indifferent to all that concerned her children, even to the loss of the *Viking*. She lived apart from them in her room, and only appeared at meal times. And when she spoke to Hulda or Joel, it was always to reproach them directly or indirectly on the subject of the lottery ticket which they had refused to part with at any price.

The offers continued to pour in. It seemed as though people had gone mad. No! It could not be possible that such a ticket was predestined not to win the prize of a hundred thousand marks. It seemed as though there was but one number in the lottery, and that was this 9672. The Englishman at Manchester, and the

American at Boston still bid against each other. The Englishman would be a few pounds in front of his rival and then he would be outbid by a few hundred dollars. The last bid had been for eight thousand marks—a state of affairs only explainable by supposing an attack of monomania, unless it had become a question of honour between America and Great Britain.

However, Hulda gave a negative reply to all these propositions, advantageous though they were—and this provoked the bitterest recriminations from Dame Hansen.

"And if I order you to give up this ticket," said she one day to her daughter. "Yes! If I order you!"

"Mother, I shall be very sorry," answered Hulda; "but I shall have to refuse."

"And it may be necessary, nevertheless."

"Why may it be necessary?" asked Joel.

Dame Hansen made no reply. She had turned ghastly pale at this simple question, and she went away muttering unintelligibly.

"There is something serious, and it must be about this Sandgoist," said Joel.

"Yes, brother. We must make up our minds for some serious trouble coming on us."

"Poor Hulda, have you not had trials enough during the last few weeks? What else can be in store for us?"

"How long Mr. Sylvius is before he comes back!" said Hulda, "when he is here I feel so much happier—"

"But what can he do for us?" asked Joel.

But what was it then that Dame Hansen would not trust to her children? What mistaken notion of self-respect kept her from telling them the reason of her anxiety? Had she done anything wrong? And why this pressure she wished to bring to bear on her daughter with regard to Ole Kamp's letter, and the value it had reached? Why did she show herself so eager after the money? Hulda and Joel were soon to know.

On the 4th of July, in the morning, Joel had taken his sister to the little chapel where Hulda went each day to pray for the lost one. He was going home with her, when, some way off under the trees, they saw Dame Hansen walking quickly towards the inn.

She was not alone. A man accompanied her, a man who seemed to be talking in a loud voice and threatening her, and whose gestures were as those of one in command.

Hulda and her brother suddenly stopped.

"Who is that man?" said Joel.

Hulda made a step or two forward.

"I recognize him," she said.

"You recognize him!"

"Yes! It is Sandgoist!"

"Sandgoist of Drammen, who came to the house while I was away?"

"Yes." ·

"And who behaved as if he were the master, and had rights over the mother—and over us, perhaps?"

"The same, brother, and these rights he has, no doubt, come to-day to enforce."

"What rights? Ah! this time I will know what the man wants here!"

Joel restrained his impatience, not without difficulty, and, followed by his sister, kept in the background.

A few minutes afterwards Dame Hansen and Sandgoist reached the door of the inn. Sandgoist crossed the threshold first. The door was shut on him and Dame Hansen, and the two were in the large room.

Joel and Hulda approached the house. They heard Sandgoist's grating voice. They stopped and listened. Dame Hansen then spoke appealingly.

"Go in," said Joel.

And Hulda with heavy heart, and Joel raging with impatience and anger, entered the large room of which the door was carefully closed.

Sandgoist was in the large armchair. He was in no way disconcerted when he caught sight of the brother and sister. He contented himself with turning his head and looking at them over his spectacles.

"Ah! There is the charming Hulda if I am not mistaken," said he, in a tone which displeased Joel.

Dame Hansen was standing before him humbly and anxiously. But she suddenly sat down and looked much disconcerted at the appearance of her children.

"And that is her brother, of course?" added Sandgoist.

"Yes, her brother," answered Joel.

And then, coming forward and stepping a couple of paces from the armchair, he continued,—

"And what can he do for you?"

Sandgoist gave him an evil look, and without rising said in a hard, cruel voice,—

"We are going to tell you, my young fellow. You have just arrived in time! I was in a hurry to see you, and if your sister is reasonable we shall end by understanding each other. But sit down, and you, too, please my girl."

Sandgoist invited them to sit down as if he were at home. And Joel told him so.

"Ah! Ah! That annoys you! You are not a particularly agreeable young man!"

"No, I am not," said Joel, "and I only accept civilities from those who have the right to offer them."

"Joel," said the dame.

"Brother! Brother!" added Hulda, with a look beseeching Joel to restrain himself.

Joel made a violent effort to recover his self-control, and resisting the temptation to throw the visitor out of the door, retired into a corner of the room.

"May I speak now?" asked Sandgoist.

An affirmative sign from Dame Hansen was all he obtained. But that seemed enough for him, and he continued,—

"This is what I have to tell you, and I hope you will all three listen, for I don't care to repeat my words."

He expressed himself, that could be seen only too well, as if he were a man who believed he could do what he chose in the matter.

"I have read in the newspapers of the adventure of a certain Ole Kamp, a young sailor of Bergen, and of a lottery ticket which he sent to his betrothed Hulda, when the *Viking* was sinking. I have also learnt that this ticket is regarded by the public as a supernatural ticket owing to the circumstances under which it was found. I have learnt besides that they attribute to it a special value in the chances of the draw. I have learnt that offers for the purchase of the ticket have been made to Hulda Hansen, and even that considerable amounts have been offered."

He was silent for a moment, and then asked,—
"Is that so?"

He waited for an answer.

"Yes," said Joel. "It is so.   What next?"

"Next?" continued Sandgoist. "This! All these offers are based on an absurd superstition, that is my opinion.   But they have been made all the same and they will increase, I suppose, up to the day of the drawing. Now I am a man of business.   I think that this is a business I can take in hand.   That is why I left Drammen to come to Dal to negotiate the handing over of this ticket, and to beg Dame Hansen to give me the preference over all other bidders."

Hulda would at once have replied to Sandgoist as she had to all the others who had made similar demands, although this was not directly addressed to her.   But Joel stopped her.

"Before answering Mr. Sandgoist," said he, "I beg to ask him if he knows to whom this ticket belongs?"

"To Hulda Hansen, I imagine!"

"Well, then, it is Hulda Hansen he should ask if she is disposed to part with it."

"My son!" said Dame Hansen.

"Let me finish, mother," continued Joel, "the ticket belonged legally only to our cousin Ole Kamp, and Ole Kamp had the right to assign it to his betrothed?"

"Undoubtedly," replied Sandgoist.

"Then you must ask Hulda Hansen if you wish to have it.'

"Be it so, Mr. Formalist.   Then I ask Hulda to hand me over this ticket, numbered 9672 which she obtained from Ole Kamp."

"Mr. Sandgoist," said she in a firm voice, "many proposals of the same character have been made to me and without effect. And I will answer you as I have answered the others. If my betrothed sent me the ticket with his last farewell, it was because he wished me to keep it, not that I should sell it. I cannot, therefore, part with it at any price."

And so saying Hulda, supposing the interview was at an end by her refusal, rose to go. At a sign from her mother she stopped. A gesture of vexation had escaped her; and Sandgoist, by the knitting of his brows and the flash in his eyes, showed that his anger had begun to master him.

"Yes, stop!" said he. "That is not your last word, and if I insist it is because I have the right to insist. I think that I explained matters badly or rather that you understood me badly. It is certain that the chance of this ticket has not been improved by its being sent from a shipwrecked man. But there is no reasoning with the infatuation of the public. There is no doubt that many people wish to possess it. They have offered to buy it, and they will still offer. I repeat, it is a matter of business, and a matter of business I propose to make it."

"It will take you some time to agree with my sister, sir," said Joel ironically. "When you talk to her of business, she answers you with sentiment."

"Merely a matter of words," said Sandgoist. "And when I have finished my explanation, you will see that if it is of advantage to me, it is also of advantage to her, and I add it will also be to the advantage of her mother, Dame Hansen, who is indirectly interested in the business."

Joel and Hulda looked at each other. Were they to learn what the dame had hitherto hidden from them?

"I do not expect," said Sandgoist, "that this ticket will be handed over for the price given for it by Ole Kamp. No! rightly or wrongly it has acquired a certain market value. And I am prepared to make a sacrifice to become its possessor."

"You have been told," said Joel, "that Hulda has already refused much better offers than you are able to make."

"Indeed," said Sandgoist, "better offers! And how do you know that?"

"Whatever they may be, my sister will refuse them, and I approve of her refusal!"

"That is it! Have I to do with Joel or Hulda Hansen?"

"My sister and I are one in this matter," answered Joel. "Know that, as you do not seem to know it."

Sandgoist, without being disconcerted, shrugged his shoulders; then, like a man sure of his arguments, he proceeded,—

"When I spoke of the price I was willing to give for this ticket, I should have told you that I could offer you advantages which, in the interest of the family, Hulda could not reject."

"Indeed."

"And now, my lad, know that I have not come to Dal to ask your sister to give me the ticket. No! A thousand times no!"

"And what, then?"

"I do not ask for it, I demand it—and I will have it!"

"And by what right do you, a stranger, speak thus in my mother's house ? "

"By the right of every man to speak as he pleases when he is at home."

"At home ?"

Joel, boiling over with rage, stepped towards Sand-goist, who, although he was not easily frightened, jumped up out of the chair.   But Hulda held back her brother, while Dame Hansen, with her face hidden in her hands, recoiled to the other end of the room.

"Brother ! look there !"

Joel stopped.   The sight of his mother paralyzed his fury.   Seeing his hesitation, Sandgoist returned to the place he had occupied.

"Yes, at home," said he in a more threatening tone. "Since her husband's death, Dame Hansen has engaged in speculations which have not succeeded.   She has lost the little fortune your father left her.   She has borrowed money from a banker at Christiania.   Penniless, she has offered this house as security for a loan of 15,000 marks, which mortgage is all in due form, and which I hold, having bought it from the original mortgagee. This house will thus be mine, and that very shortly, if I am not paid when my notice expires."

"When will that notice expire ?" asked Joel.

"On the 20th of July, in eighteen hours," answered Sandgoist.   "And then, whether you like it or not, I shall here be at home."

"You will not be at home until then, and then only if you have not been paid off," replied Joel.   "And I forbid you to speak as you have done before my mother and sister."

"He defies me!" exclaimed Sandgoist. "And does his mother defy me?"

"Speak, mother," said Joel, moving towards the dame, and trying to unclasp Hulda's hand.

"Joel! My brother!" exclaimed Hulda. "In pity for her! I beseech you—be calm!"

Dame Hansen, with her head bowed, dare not look at her son. It was only too true that a few years after her husband's death she had been tempted to try and increase her fortune by risky speculations. The little money she had was speedily squandered. Soon she had to take refuge in various loans. And now a mortgage on the house had passed into the hands of this Sandgoist of Drammen, a man without any heart at all, a well-known money-lender, detested throughout the country. Dame Hansen had seen him for the first time the day he came to Dal to value the house.

This then was the secret which weighed on her life! This was the explanation of her behaviour, and why she lived apart as if she wished to hide herself from her children. This is what she had never dared tell to those whose future she had jeopardized.

Hulda dared hardly believe what she had just heard. Yes! Sandgoist was, indeed, in a position to do as he pleased. The ticket he wanted to-day would be value-less in fifteen days, and if she did not hand it over it meant ruin, the house sold, the Hansens homeless and penniless. That was the misery of it!

Hulda dared not lift her eyes to Joel. But Joel was too angry to listen to the menacing future. He saw only Sandgoist, and if that man spoke again as he had just done, he would not be able to control himself.

"Brother! Look there!"

Page 137.

Sandgoist, knowing he was master of the situation, became even more insulting and imperious.

"I want the ticket, and I will have it," he repeated. "In exchange I do not offer a price it is impossible to fix, but to offer to postpone the notice of the procedure for a year—for two years! You can fix the date yourself, Hulda."

Hulda, with her heart wrung with anguish, knew not what to say. Her brother answered for her,—

"Ole Kamp's ticket cannot be sold by Hulda Hansen. My sister refuses, notwithstanding your pretensions and your threats! And now, get out!"

"Get out!" said Sandgoist. "Well, no! I shall not get out! And if the offer I have made is not enough— I will go further. Yes! Give me the ticket and I will give—give—"

It was evident that Sandgoist had an irresistible desire to possess this ticket, it was evident that he thought he could make something out of the business, for he went and sat down at the table, where there was some paper with a pen and ink, and then after a moment,—

"That is what I will give you!" said he.

It was a receipt in full for the sum due by Dame Hansen, and for which she had given the mortgage over the house.

Dame Hansen, with her hands together, beseechingly bent almost to the ground, and looked imploringly at her daughter.

"And now," said Sandgoist, "the ticket. I will have it. I will have it to-day—now! I will not leave Dal without! I will have it, Hulda! I will!"

Sandgoist approached the girl as though he would search her and snatch the ticket away from her.

This was more than Joel could stand, particularly when he heard Hulda exclaim,—

"Brother! brother!"

"Get out!" he said.

And when Sandgoist refused to stir, he was about to hurl himself at him when Hulda intervened,—

"Mother! here is the ticket!"

Dame Hansen eagerly clutched it, and while she exchanged it for Sandgoist's receipt, Hulda fell senseless on the chair.

"Hulda! Hulda!" said Joel, "take it back! Ah! my sister what have you done?"

"What has she done?" answered Dame Hansen. "What has she done? Yes, I am the guilty one! For my children's sake I thought to increase their father's fortune! And I have ruined their future! I have brought misery on the house! But Hulda has saved us all! See what she has done! Thanks, Hulda! Thanks!"

Sandgoist still remained, as Joel saw.

"You—here—yet!" he exclaimed.

And rushing up to him he gripped him by the shoulders, and in spite of his struggles and his shouts threw him head-first out of the house.

CHAPTER XV.

SYLVIUS HOG returned to Dal in the course of the next evening. He said nothing of his journey. Nobody knew of his visit to Bergen. If the search he had instituted resulted in nothing, he wished to keep it secret from the Hansen family. Any letter or despatch coming from Bergen or Christiania would be addressed to him personally at the inn, where he proposed to await events. Did he still hope? Yes, but it would not do to say so, for hope was only a presentiment.

As soon as he returned, the professor had no difficulty in seeing that something serious had happened in his absence. The manner of Joel and Hulda showed clearly that an explanation had taken place between them and their mother. Had some new misfortune fallen on the Hansen family?

Sylvius Hog was deeply affected. He felt for brother and sister so paternal an affection that he could not have been more attached to them had they been his own children. How much he had missed them during his short absence—and, perhaps, how much they had missed him!

"They will tell me," he said to himself; "they will tell me. Am I not one of the family?"

Yes! Sylvius Hog considered that he now had the right to interfere with the private matters of his young friends and to know why Joel and Hulda appeared more unhappy than they did when he went away. He had not to wait long to learn.

In fact they were only too glad to confide in this excellent man, whom they loved with such filial affection. For two days they felt themselves abandoned; for Sylvius Hog had not told them where he was going. Never had hours appeared so long. For them the journey had no connection with the search for the *Viking*, and it would never have occurred to them that the professor had kept his destination secret to spare them the final disillusion in case of ill-success.

And now his presence was more than ever necessary to them. How they longed to come to him, and ask his advice, and listen to his cheery voice! But could they dare to tell him what had passed between them and the Drammen money-lender, and how Dame Hansen had jeopardized the future of the house? What would Sylvius Hog think when he learnt that the ticket was not in Hulda's possession, when he knew that Dame Hansen had used it to pay off a pitiless creditor?

He was to know nevertheless. Who began to speak about it—Sylvius Hog, or Joel, or Hulda—no one knew. But that is of no consequence. What is certain is that the professor soon knew all about it. He knew the difficulty in which Dame Hansen and her children had been placed. In fifteen days the usurer would have turned them out of the inn at Dal unless his debt had been satisfied by the surrender of the ticket.

Sylvius Hog had listened to the sad story as told him by Joel in his sister's presence.

"You should not have given up the ticket!" he exclaimed. "No, you should not have given it up!"

" What could I do, Mr. Sylvius?" said Hulda in great trouble.

" Well! Perhaps! You could not help yourself! If I had only been there !"

And what would you have done if you had only been there, Professor Sylvius Hog? He said nothing, and continued,—

" Yes, my dear Hulda ; yes, Joel. In short, you have done all you could. But what makes me so angry is that Sandgoist should profit by the superstitious infatuation of the people. That he should make something out of the supernatural value they have attributed to Ole's ticket. But to believe that this number 9672 will be necessarily favoured by chance is ridiculous, absurd! But I don't think I should have given him the ticket; after refusing it to Sandgoist, Hulda would have done better in refusing it to her mother."

To this brother and sister could say nothing. In giving the ticket to Dame Hansen, Hulda had obeyed a filial sentiment for which she could not be blamed. The sacrifice she had made was not the sacrifice of the chance more or less uncertain of the ticket being drawn in the lottery at Christiania, it was the sacrifice of the last wishes of Ole Kamp ; it was the giving away of the last keepsake from her betrothed. But there was no going back ; Sandgoist held the ticket. It belonged to him. He would put it up to be bid for. A rascally money-lender would make money out of this touching farewell from the shipwrecked man! No! Sylvius Hog could not stand that!

And so that very day Sylvius Hog asked for a little conversation with Dame Hansen—a conversation which could not alter the state of affairs, but which it was inevitable should take place. He found he had to deal with a woman who had considerably more good sense than feeling.

"And so you blame me, Mr. Hog?" said she, after listening to all the professor had to say.

"Certainly I do."

"If you blame me for venturing into such foolish speculation, and risking my children's fortune, you are right. But if you blame me for doing what I did to free myself, you are wrong. What do you say to that?"

"Nothing."

"Seriously, how could I refuse Sandgoist's offer, which, after all, was to pay me fifteen thousand marks for a ticket whose value is based on nothing? I again ask you. Could I refuse?"

"Yes, and no, Dame Hansen."

"It is not yes and no, Mr. Hog; it is no. Situated as you know, if the future had not been so threatening —by my fault, I admit—I could have understood Hulda's refusal. Yes! I could have understood that she would not part with the ticket she had received from Ole Kamp at any price. But when there came the question of being in a few days turned out of the house in which my husband died, and in which my children were born, I do not see—and neither would you, Mr. Hog, had you been in my place—how I could have acted otherwise."

"Yes, I would, Dame Hansen."

"And what would you have done?"

"I would have done everything rather than sacrifice the ticket which my daughter had received under such circumstances!"

" Did the circumstances make it any the better ? "

" Neither you, nor I, nor anybody can say."

" We can say, Mr. Hog! The ticket is but one which has 999,999 chances to lose against one to win. Do you think it has any more value for having been found in a bottle picked up at sea ? "

To this question Sylvius Hog found it rather embarrassing to reply. And so he returned to the sentimental side of the matter.

" The position is this. Ole Kamp, at the moment of his shipwreck, gave away all that he had in this world ! He even asked her to be there on the day of the drawing, with this ticket, in case any lucky chance should follow it ; and now the ticket is not Hulda's ! "

" Had Ole Kamp been home," answered Dame Hansen, " he would not have hesitated to give it up to Sandgoist."

" That is possible," said Sylvius Hog. " But he alone had the right to do it. And what will you say, if he is not dead, if he has not been lost in the wreck, if he comes back, to-morrow—to-day ? "

" He will not come back," said Dame Hansen, " Ole is dead, Mr. Hog ; dead ! "

" You do not know, Dame Hansen," exclaimed the professor, with a truly extraordinary emphasis of conviction. " An important search has begun for recovering some traces of the wreck. It may succeed—yes, succeed before the drawing of this lottery. You have no right to say that Ole Kamp is dead so long as there exist no proofs that he perished in the loss of the *Viking*. If I do not speak with such assurance to your children, it is because I do not wish to give them hopes which may be

disappointed. But to you, Dame Hansen, I say what I
think! And that Ole is dead I do not believe! No!
I do not believe it!"

On the ground to which the contest had been shifted,
Dame Hansen could not argue with the professor, and
so she remained silent. Like all the Norwegians, she
was in reality somewhat superstitious after all, and so
she bowed her head as if Ole Kamp was ready to appear
before her.

"Anyhow," said Sylvius Hog, "before you disposed
of Hulda's ticket there was one very simple thing to do
which you did not do."

"And what was that, sir ?"

"You should have appealed to your friends, to the
friends of your family. They would not have refused
to take over Sandgoist's mortgage by advancing you
the money to pay him off and taking the same security."

"I have no friends, Mr. Hog, to whom I could have
applied in such a matter."

"If you have none, Dame Hansen, I know of one at
least who would have had no hesitation in helping you,
as an act of gratitude."

"And who is he?

"Sylvius Hog, member of the Storthing."

Dame Hansen could say nothing, and she contented
herself with making a bow to the professor.

"But what is done, is done—unfortunately!" said
Sylvius Hog. "I shall be much obliged, Dame Hansen,
if you will say nothing about this conversation to your
children!"

And he left her.

The professor resumed his usual routine, and began

his daily walks. For a few hours he walked with Joel and Hulda in the neighbourhood of Dal without going too far away, so as not to fatigue the girl. Then he attended to his correspondence. He wrote letters to Bergen, to Christiania. He stimulated the zeal of all who were now engaged in the good work of seeking the *Viking*. All his existence was concentrated on this one thought ; to find Ole, to find Ole !

He even thought it best to go away for twenty-four hours for an object which doubtless had something to do with the Hansens. But he kept it secret, as he did the other matter.

Hulda's health improved but slowly. The poor girl only lived in remembrance of her lover, and the hope which mingled with the remembrance grew feebler day by day. And this, although she had near her the two people whom she loved best in this world and one of whom never ceased to encourage her. But was that enough for her? Was it not necessary to distract her thoughts at any price? And could they distract the thoughts, which seemed to have taken entire possession of her—thoughts which seemed bound as by a chain of iron to the wreck of the *Viking?*

The 12th of July came, and in four days there would be drawn the lottery of the Schools of Christiania.

It need hardly be mentioned that the speculation entered on by Sandgoist had been brought to the public notice. The journals announced, at his instigation, that "the celebrated and providential ticket," being the number 9672, was now in the hands of Mr. Sandgoist of Drammen, and that the ticket was on sale for the highest bidder. And if Mr. Sandgoist was the possessor of the aforesaid ticket it was because he had bought it very dearly from Hulda Hansen.

As may be supposed, this announcement made the girl sink very much in the public estimation. What! Hulda, for the sake of the high price, had sold the ticket of the shipwrecked man, the ticket of her betrothed! She had made money out of his last keepsake!

But a paragraph that appeared very opportunely in the *Morgenblad* informed its readers of the true state of the case. It stated what was the true story of the ticket getting into Sandgoist's hands. And so the money-lender fell under the public reprobation, as the heartless creditor who had had no compunction in making use o the misfortunes of the Hansen family for his own gain. And so it happened by general consent that the offers which were made while Hulda held the ticket were not renewed to the new owner. It seemed that the ticket had lost its supernatural value now that Sandgoist had soiled it with his hands. The money-lender had, after all, done a very bad stroke of business, and it seemed as though the famous No. 9672 would prove a dead loss.

Neither Hulda nor Joel knew of what was going on. It would have been painful for them to know they were mixed up in a matter which had taken so mercantile a turn in the hands of the money-lender.

The 12th of July came, and in the evening there arrived a letter addressed to Professor Sylvius Hog.

The letter had been sent on by the Shipping Board, and contained another which was dated from Christiansand, a little port situated at the entrance to the Gulf of Christiania. Doubtless it contained no news to Sylvius

Hog, for he folded it up, and said nothing about it either to Joel or his sister.

Only as he was bidding them good night, he said,—

"You know, my children, that in three days the lottery is to be drawn. Are you going to be there?"

"What will be the use?" asked Hulda.

"Well," said the professor, "Ole wished his betrothed to be there, and he said so in the last few lines he wrote. And I think you should accede to his last request."

"But Hulda no longer has the ticket," answered Joel. "And who knows into whose hands it has fallen."

"It does not matter," said Sylvius Hog. "I wish you to come with me to Christiania."

"You wish us to come, Mr. Sylvius?" asked Hulda.

"It is not I, dear Hulda, it is Ole who wishes you to come, and Ole you should obey."

"Sister, Mr. Sylvius is right," said Joel. "Yes! it must be so! When do you start, Mr. Sylvius?"

"To-morrow at day-break, and may St. Olaf watch over us!"

CHAPTER XVI.

IN the morning the carriole of Overseer Lengling bore off Sylvius Hog and Hulda, seated side by side in its little painted box. As we know, there was no place for Joel; and so he walked by the side of the horse, which shook its head gaily between the shafts. The nine miles between Dal and Mœl were nothing to this sturdy walker.

The carriole went along the charming valley of Vestfjorddal, by the left bank of the Maan—a valley narrow and shady, watered by a thousand leaping cascades falling from all heights. At every turn of the winding road, the summit of Gousta appeared and disappeared, marked with its two bright spots of snow.

The sky was clear, the weather magnificent; the air not too keen, the sun not too hot.

One thing was noticeable, and that was, that as soon as Sylvius Hog left the house at Dal, he seemed to cheer up considerably. Doubtless much of this was mere pretence, so that the journey might really prove a change for Hulda and Joel.

In two hours and a half they would reach Mœl, at the end of Lake Tinn. There they would leave the carriole; for the road henceforth would be on the bosom of the lake. Thenceforward they would have to go by "vands-kyde," that is to say, by relays of boats.

The carriole stopped near the little church of the hamlet, at the foot of the five-hundred-feet fall. This waterfall is visible for a fifth of its descent; and disappears in a deep crevasse in the mountain before being absorbed by the lake.

Two boatmen were at the end of the beach. A birch-bark boat of unstable equilibrium, which did not allow of the slightest movement on the part of the travellers, was ready to start. All they could do was to fervently wish for a fine passage.

"You are not very tired, Joel?" asked the professor as soon as he had left the carriole.

"No, Mr. Sylvius. Am I not used to long tramps all over Tellemarken?"

"That is so. Tell me, do you know the nearest way from Mœl to Christiania?"

"Quite well. When you get to the end of the lake at Tinoset—I don't know whether we shall find a carriole, if you have not sent on the 'forbuds,' to bespeak relays as they do in these parts—"

"All right, my lad. I saw about that. I don't want you to walk all the way from Dal to Christiania."

"I'll do it if it's necessary," said Joel.

"It is not necessary. Let us have your road now."

"Well, when you get to Tinoset, you keep along by Lake Fol through Vik and Bolkesjö, so as to reach Möse, and then through Konsberg, Hangsund, and Drammen. If we travel night and day we may get to Christiania to-morrow afternoon."

"Very well, Joel. I see you know the country; and it is a pleasant road!"

"It is the shortest."

"Well, I don't care about the shortest. You see," said the professor, "I know another which only makes a difference of a few hours! And that you know, although you don't say so!"

"Which is that?"

"The one through Bamble."

"Through Bamble."

"Yes, Bamble, Mr. Innocent! Bamble, where there lives a farmer named Helmboë, and his daughter Siegfrid."

"Mr. Sylvius!"

"That is the way we will go, passing round Lake Fol to the south instead of to the north. We can get to Konsberg that way?"

"That will do as well, and perhaps better," said Joel, with a smile.

"Thank you, for my brother's sake," said Hulda.

"And for yours also, little Hulda, for I imagine it will do you good to call in on your friend Siegfrid."

They were soon in the boat, seated on a heap of green leaves in the stern. The two boatmen, rowing and steering, pushed off.

As they left the bank, Lake Tinn began to curve towards Hækenös, a small gaard of two or three houses, built on the rocky promontory, bathed by the narrow fjord into which flow peaceably the waters of the Maan. The lake is still much shut in ; but gradually the background of mountains recedes and their height is only apparent when the boat, looking like a bird, glides along by their foot. Here and there a dozen isles or islets emerge, barren or verdant. On the surface of the lake float a few trunks of trees, untrimmed and boasting a

tail of sawdust fallen into the lake from the neighbouring sawmills.

In three hours the travellers arrived at Tinoset. As
Sylvius Hog had said to Joel, a vehicle was waiting for
them on the shore. In view of the journey, which he
had for some time decided upon in his own mind, he had
written to Mr. Bennett, of Christiania, to provide the
means of travelling without delay or fatigue. That is
why, on the day stated, an old caleche came to Tinoset
with a well-furnished hamper of provisions.

Tinoset is situated almost at the end of Lake Tinn.
There by a fine cascade the Maan is precipitated into
the lower valley, where it resumes its regular course.
The horses were ready and had been put to, and the
vehicle was soon off towards Bamble.

At this time this was the only way of travelling in
Norway in general, and in Tellemarken in particular ;
and perhaps the railways are not unregretted by the
tourists who remember the national carriole and the
caleches of Mr. Bennett ?

Joel, of course, thoroughly knew that portion of the
bailiwick which he had often traversed between Dal and
Bamble. It was eight o'clock in the evening when the
travellers arrived at Bamble. They were not expected,
but the farmer Helmboë made them none the less
welcome. Siegfrid tenderly embraced her friend, whom
she found very pale after her many sorrows ; and for a
few minutes the girls remained by themselves talking
over their troubles.

"My dear Hulda," said Siegfrid, "you must not let
your sorrow overcome you. I have not lost confidence
yet. Why give up all hope of again seeing your poor

Ole ? We see in the papers that they are still looking
for the *Viking !* The search will succeed ! I am sure
Mr. Sylvius still hopes. Hulda—my dear—I beseech
you—don't despair."

Hulda's only answer was to weep, and Siegfrid clasped
her to her bosom.

Ah ! what joy would have reigned in the house of
farmer Helmboë, among these good, simple folks, if all
this little world had had the right to be happy !

"And so you are going straight to Christiania ? "
asked the farmer of Sylvius Hog.

" Yes, Mr. Helmboë."

" To be present at the drawing of the lottery ! "

" Certainly."

" What is the good of that, now Ole Kamp's ticket
is in the hands of that scoundrel Sandgoist ? " '

" It is Ole's wish," answered the professor, " and we
must respect it."

" They say the Drammen money-lender has not found
a purchaser for the ticket which cost him so much."

" They do, Mr. Helmboë."

" Good ! He has only got what he deserves, the
scoundrel,—the rascal, Mr. Hog ! The scoundrel ! Serve
him right ! "

" Exactly so, Mr. Helmboë ; serve him right ! "

Naturally they had some supper at the farm. Neither
Siegfrid nor her father would allow them to leave until
they had accepted the invitation. But they could not
stay long if they wished to make up the few hours they
had lost by their call at Bamble. And so at nine o'clock
the horses were put to by one of the farm lads of the
gaard

"The next time I come," said Sylvius Hog, "I will remain six hours at the table if you like ! But now I must ask you to substitute for the dessert a warm shake of the hand and a kiss from the fair Siegfrid to my little Hulda."

And that was done ; and they set out.

In that light latitude the twilight lasts for several hours ; and the horizon remained visible long after sunset, for the air was clear.

It is a splendid road and beautifully varied that leads from Bamble to Kongsberg going by Hitterdal and the south of Lake Fol. It crosses the entire southern portion of Tellemarken through the towns and hamlets and the gaards in their neighbourhood.

An hour after the departure, Sylvius Hog without pulling up sighted the church of Hetterdal, a very curious old edifice capped by pinnacles rising one over the other without any regard to the regularity of the lines. It is all built of wood, with walls of jointed beams and weather-boarding up to the extreme point of the highest tower, this pile of pepper-boxes is, it appears, a venerable and venerated monument of the Scandinavian architecture of the thirteenth century.

Then night gradually came on—one of those nights impregnated with the last rays of the day, which towards the first hour of the morning die out in the dawn.

Joel, seated on the box in front, was absorbed in his reflections. Hulda remained deep in thought at the back of the carriage. A few words were exchanged between Sylvius Hog and the postillion, in which the professor requested him to urge on his horses. Then nothing was heard but the bells of the horses, the crack-

ing] of the whip, and the grinding of the wheels on
the deeply-rutted ground.   All the night they kept on
without changing.

It was unnecessary to stop at Listhüs, an un-
comfortable station hidden in a ring of fir-clad hills
which in its turn is encircled by a second ring of
wild and barren mountains.   They passed also Tiness,
a small picturesque gaard where a few houses are perched
on a pile of stones.   The caleche rolled along rapidly
with its clinking ironwork, its rattling bolts and stretching springs.   The driver could not be growled at—a
good old fellow who slept half the time he was whipping
at the leaders.   Mechanically he favoured the horses
with his whip-strokes, not because they were obstinate,
and by preference the left horse received the most liberal
allowance, for the right horse belonged to the postillion
while the left belonged to his cousin at the gaard.

At five o'clock in the morning Sylvius Hog opened
his eyes, stretched his arms, and took a long, deep
breath of the penetrating perfume of the firs which scented
the atmosphere.

They were at Kongsberg.   The carriage crossed the
bridge over the Laagen, and stopped a little beyond,
having passed the church not far from the fall of
Larbrö.

"My friends," said Sylvius Hog, "if you like we will
only change horses here.   It is too early for breakfast.
Better make a halt at Drammen.   There we can give
ourselves a good feed, so as to economize the good things
of Mr. Bennett."

This was agreed to, and Joel contented himself with a
small glass of brandy at the Mines Hotel.   Then in a

quarter of an hour the horses arrived, and the journey was resumed.

On leaving the village the carriage had to ascend a steepish slope cut out of the flank of the mountain. For a moment the high pylones of the silver mines at Kongsberg were outlined against the sky. Then the whole horizon disappeared behind a curtain of immense pine-trees, dark as caves, in which neither the heat nor the light of the sun ever penetrated.

The wooden town of Hangsund furnished another team to the caleche. Soon they were on long roads barred by gates which cost them five or six shillings as toll for opening : a fertile region where trees abounded resembling weeping willows as their branches bent beneath the weight of the fruit. Then the valley began to become mountainous as they neared Drammen.

At noon the town, situated on one of the arms of the Christiania fjord, showed them its two long streets bordered with painted houses, and its harbour, always very animated, where the rafts of wood leave but little space for the ships which come to load with the products of the north.

The carriage stopped before the Scandinavian Hotel. The landlord, an important personage with a white beard and the air of a doctor, appeared at the door of his establishment. With that keenness of perception which distinguishes innkeepers in all parts of the world, he remarked,—

"I should not be surprised if these gentlemen and that lady would like a little breakfast ? "

"You need not be surprised," said Sylvius Hog, " and you can let us have it as soon as possible."

"This instant."

The breakfast was soon ready, and proved very acceptable. It consisted chiefly of a certain fish from the fjord stuffed with sweet herbs ; and the professor ate it with evident pleasure.

In an hour and a half the carriage, horsed by a fresh team, had left the Scandinavian Hotel and was proceeding at a gentle trot along the main street of Drammen.

But as they were passing a house of unattractive aspect which contrasted unfavourably with the gay colour of its neighbours, Joel could not resist a gesture of repulsion as he exclaimed,—

"Sandgoist !"

"Oh, that is Mr. Sandgoist !" said the professsor. "Well, I don't think much of his looks ! "

It was Sandgoist. He was smoking at his door. Whether he recognized Joel on the seat in front we cannot say, for the carriage speedily disappeared between the hills of balks and the mountains of planks.

Beyond the road bordered with service-trees, loaded with their coral fruit, the carriage drove on through a thick forest of pines which borders the Paradise Valley, a magnificent depression of the ground with the farthest stages rising to the very limits of the horizon. Hundreds of hills then appeared, most of them covered with a villa or a gaard. Then as evening approached, when the caleche began to descend towards the sea, by the side of the huge meadows farms appeared with their red houses standing out sharply from their blackish-green curtains of trees. Finally the travellers reached the fjord of Christiania framed with its picturesque hills, with its innumerable creeks, its miniature harbours and their wooden piers, at which the vessels and steam omnibuses call.

At eleven o'clock at night, just as the last rays of the twilight were fading away, the old caleche entered the town, not without some clatter as it rolled through the deserted streets.

According to the orders of Sylvius Hog they drove to the Hotel du Nord, where Hulda and Joel alighted and took possession of the rooms which had been engaged for them in advance. Then the professor, with an affectionate good night, regained his old house, where his old nurse Kate and his old servant Fink were waiting for him with a no less old impatience.

CHAPTER XVII.

CHRISTIANIA, though a large city for Norway, would
be only a small town in England or France. Were it
not for the frequent fires, it would be to-day as it was
built in the eleventh century. In reality it dates only from
the year 1624, when it was rebuilt by King Christian.
D'Opsolö it was then called, becoming Christiania from
the feminized name of the royal architect. It is a regular
town, with large streets, dull and straight as if ruled,
with houses of white stone or red bricks. In the centre
of a tolerable garden there stands the royal palace, the
Oscarslot, a large quadrangular building without any
style, although it claims to be in the Ionian style. Here
and there are a few churches, in which the beauties of art
are not likely to disturb the faithful. There are many
Government buildings and public establishments, to say
nothing of a grand bazaar in the form of a rotunda
where all the foreign and native products are sold.

In all this there is nothing curious. But what can be
admired without reservation is the position of the town
in the centre of its ring of mountains, which with their
varied aspect form so superb a frame. Almost flat in
the new and wealthy quarters, it rises only to form a sort
of kasbah covered with irregular houses, where there
vegetates a needy population in huts of wood, and huts
of brick, whose gorgeous colours astonish the eye more
than they charm it.

It need not be supposed that the word kasbah, restricted to African towns, is out of place in a city of the north of Europe ; for has not Christiania, down near the harbour, the quarters of Tunis, Morocco, and Algiers ? And if these have no Tunisians, Moroccans, or Algerians, their floating population is not much better. Like all towns rising from the shore into the green hills, Christiania is extremely picturesque. It is not unjust to compare its fjord to the Bay of Naples. Like the banks of Sorrento and Castellamare, its banks are dotted with villas and cottages half-hidden in the almost black verdure of the pines, and wrapped in those light vapours which in the northern regions have received the name of the " flou."

Sylvius Hog had at last returned to Christiania. It is true the return had taken place under unforeseen circumstances, in the middle of his interrupted journey. Well, he would leave it to try again another year. Now he thought only of Joel and Hulda Hansen. If he had not brought them to his house, it was because he had not two rooms to receive them. Assuredly old Fink and old Kate would have made them welcome. But there was no time to get ready. The professor had therefore taken them to the Hotel du Nord, and given them a particular introduction ; and a recommendation from Sylvius Hog, member of the Storthing, was worth something.

But while the professor had bespoken for his guests the same attention he would have himself, he had not given their names. To keep *incognito* at first seemed to him to be only prudent. We know what rumour had done for the girl, and how it had annoyed her. It was best to say nothing of her arrival at Christiania.

It had been agreed that in the morning Sylvius Hog would not call upon the Hansens until nearly noon.

The professor had in fact some business to do, which might take him all the morning, and he would rejoin Hulda and Joel as soon as he had finished. He would not then leave them, but would remain with them until the drawing of the lottery, which was to take place in three hours.

As soon as Joel was up, he went to his sister Hulda, who was already dressed and awaiting him in her room. With the object of distracting her thoughts, Joel proposed they should go for a walk. Hulda did not care to disoblige him, and the two went out into the town.

It was a Sunday. Contrary to what is generally the case in the cities of the north on holidays, when the number of people in the streets is very small, there was a considerable amount of animation. Not only had the citizens not left the town for the country, but crowds of people were pouring in from the rural districts. The Lake Mjosen railway, which serves the environs of the capital, was running special trains, so great was the number of sightseers and ticket-holders attracted by the popular lottery of the Schools of Christiania.

Joel and Hulda, on leaving the Hotel du Nord, found their way down to the quays at the eastern side of the bay. There the crowd was not so great, except in the public-houses, where beer and brandy were cooling the throats of such as seemed to be in a permanent state of thirst.

While the brother and sister were walking among the

sheds, the rows of casks, and the heaps of cases of all kinds, the ships moored to the wharves or anchored in the stream attracted their attention. Were there not amongst them some ships from Bergen whither the *Viking* would never return ?

"Ole ! my poor Ole !" murmured Hulda. And Joel led the way from the bay up into the higher quarters of the town. There in the streets and squares they over- heard many things in which they were interested.

"Yes," said one, "they offered ten thousand marks for No. 9672 !"

"Ten thousand !" said another. "I heard twenty thousand, and even more."

"Mr. Vanderbilt, of New York, has offered thirty thousand."

"Messrs. Baring, of London, have offered forty thousand."

"Messrs. Rothschild, of London, have offered sixty thousand."

We know what popular exaggeration is like. At this rate the prices offered would soon have amounted to more than the prize.

But if the speakers were not agreed as to the amount of the offers made to Hulda Hansen, the crowd were strangely unanimous in condemning the Drammen money-lender.

"What a scoundrel that Sandgoist must be to have had no pity on those poor people."

"Yes, he is well known in Tellemarken ; and it is not his first attempt."

"They say he cannot get rid of the ticket now."

"No ! No one will buy it."

"That is not surprising. In Hulda Hansen's hands the ticket would have been good!"

"Evidently in Sandgoist's hands it would be worthless."

"And all the better! He would get nothing, and lose the fifteen thousand marks it cost him."

"But if the beggar wins?"

"He! Not likely!"

"That would be unfair! Anyhow he had better not come to the drawing."

"No! it might be the worse for him!"

Such is a summary of the popular opinion as to Sandgoist. We know also that from prudence or some other motive he had no intention of assisting at the draw, as the night before we saw him at his house-door in Drammen.

Hulda was much agitated, and Joel, feeling her arm tremble in his, hurried along without waiting to hear more than he could help, fearing that they might be recognized and cheered by their friends in the crowd.

They had hoped to meet Sylvius Hog in the town, but saw nothing of him, though, from a few words they overheard, they knew that his return to Christiania was already known to the people. Since the morning he has been seen hurrying about with a busy look on his face, as though he had no time to answer questions, first down about the harbour, and then about the offices of the Shipping Board.

Joel had only to ask the first bystander he came across where Professor Sylvius Hog lived to be immediately informed. But he did not do this for fear of being indiscreet and as the meeting had been arranged to take place at the hotel, he thought it best to return there.

And this is what Hulda asked Joel to do about half-past ten, for she felt tired, and the scraps of conversation she had overheard had done her no good.

They went back to the Hotel du Nord, and there she went to her room and awaited the professor's return, while Joel remained downstairs in the reading-room. There he occupied himself in mechanically running over the Christiania newspapers.

Suddenly he grew pale, his look became troubled, and the journal he held fell from his hands.

In a number of the *Morgenblad*, among the shipping intelligence, there was the following message from Newfoundland :—

"The despatch boat *Telegraf* has visited the presumed site of the wreck of the *Viking*, and found no trace of it. Her investigations on the Greenland coast have been unsuccessful. It can be considered certain that there is no survivor of the crew of the *Viking*."

CHAPTER XVIII.

" GOOD morning, Mr. Bennett!   It is always a pleasure to shake hands with you."

" And it is always an honour—for me, Mr. Hog ! "

" Honour, pleasure, pleasure, honour," said the professor gaily.   " One is as good as the other."

" I see your trip through central Norway is successfully completed."

" It is not completed, but it is finished," said the professor,—" for this year at least."

" Well, Mr. Hog, tell me something about those good people you became acquainted with at Dal."

" Good people, in truth, Mr. Bennett.   The word suits them in both senses."

" From what the papers say, they are much to be pitied."

" Very much, Mr. Bennett.   I never knew misfortune fall more heavily on people."

" After the affair of the *Viking*, the business of that abominable Sandgoist ! "

" Just so."

"After all, Hulda Hansen did not do so badly in handing the ticket over."

" Why not ?   Do you think so ? "

" To get fifteen thousand marks for a *quasi*-certainty of getting nothing—"

"Ah, Mr Bennett, you talk like a practical man, a merchant as you are. But if you take another view it becomes a matter of sentiment, and sentiment you cannot express in figures."

"Exactly, Mr. Hog; but allow me to say that it is very probable your friend would have got nothing for her sentiment."

"How do you know?"

"Why, just think! What did the ticket represent? One chance in a million!"

"Quite so; and a very poor chance, Mr. Bennett!"

"And so reaction has set in after the infatuation of the first days, and they say that this Sandgoist, who only bought the ticket to speculate with, cannot find a buyer!"

"It would seem so, Mr. Bennett."

"But if the money-lender were to win the prize it would be a scandal."

"A scandal, certainly; the word is not too strong—truly, a scandal."

And chatting thus the professor walked through the shops, or we might say the bazaar, of Mr. Bennett, so well known in Christiania and throughout Norway. And what cannot be found in these stores? Travelling carriages, carrioles by the dozen, boxes of provisions, baskets of wines, stocks of preserves, clothes and implements for tourists, and even guides for tours in the farthest districts of Finmarken, and the land of the Lapps, even to the North Pole! And that is not all. Does not Mr. Bennett offer to the lovers of natural history, specimens of the rocks and minerals, and of the birds, insects and reptiles? And—and it is as well to

know it—where can you find an assortment of jewels
and local *bric-a-brac* more complete than that in his glass
cases? And so this gentleman is the Providence of
tourists desirous of visiting Scandinavia. He is the
universal man whom Christiania could not spare.

"And by the way, Mr. Hog," he said, "you found
at Tinoset the carriage you asked me to have there?"

"When I ordered it I was certain it would be
there."

"You flatter me, Mr. Hog; but according to your
letter you had three people—"

"There were three."

"And these people?"

"They came yesterday evening in good health, and
they are now waiting for me at the Hotel du Nord where
I am going to them."

"Are they—?"

"Exactly, Mr. Bennett, they are— And I hope you
will say nothing about it. I do not wish their arrival to
be noised abroad."

"Poor girl!"

"Yes, she has suffered much."

"And you wished her to be present at the drawing of
the lottery, although she no longer has the ticket she
received from her betrothed."

"It is not I who wished her to! It was Ole Kamp!
And to you, as to every one else—I repeat it!—the last
words of Ole must be obeyed!"

"What you do is always well done, dear Mr. Hog."

"Compliments, Mr. Bennett?"

"No; but it is very lucky for her that the Hansen
family came in your way."

" And very lucky for me that they came in mine."

" You always had a good heart."

" Mr. Bennett, if we are obliged to have a heart, it may as well be a good one."

And with what an excellent smile did Sylvius Hog make this reply to the worthy merchant!

" And now, Mr. Bennett, do not think I came here to exchange congratulations. I came with another motive.

"Well, I am at your service."

"You know—is it not so ?—that without the help of Joel and Hulda Hansen, the Rjukanfos, if it had given me up at all, would have surrendered me as a corpse. I should not then have the pleasure of seeing you."

"Yes! yes! I know!" answered Mr. Bennett. "The newspapers told us of your adventure. And, I think, those young people ought to win the grand prize."

" So do I," said Sylvius Hog ; " but as that is now impossible, I should like my little Hulda to return to Dal with a present—a keepsake."

" That is what I call a good idea, Mr. Hog."

" Then, perhaps, you will help me to choose something suitable ?"

" Willingly," said Mr. Bennett.

And he asked the professor to follow him into the shop where the native jewellery was displayed. Would not a piece of Norwegian jewellery be the most charming souvenir that she could take away from Christiania and the wonderful stores of Mr. Bennett ?

So thought Sylvius Hog, for whom the complaisant gentleman hastened to open all his glass cases.

" Look here," said he ; " I am not much of a judge, and I'll trust to your taste, Mr. Bennett."

"We will see, Mr. Hog."

There was an assortment of Swedish and Norwegian jewellery of very complex workmanship, generally more precious for the work than the material.

"What is that?" asked the professor.

"That is a double jewel with movable tassels whose colours are very beautiful."

"Very pretty," said the professor, balancing the jewel at the tip of his little finger. "Put it aside, Mr. Bennett, and let us look at something else."

"Bracelets or necklaces?"

"A little of all, if you like, a little of all! Ah! that?"

"They are shields, worn in pairs on the bodice. See the effect of the copper on the background of folded linen. It is very good taste, and not very high in price."

"It looks charming, Mr. Bennett. Put that aside."

"There is only one thing, and that is that these things are only worn by young brides on the wedding day—and that—"

"By Saint Olaf, you are right! you are right! Poor Hulda! Unfortunately it is not Ole who gives her this present, but I; and it is not to a sweetheart that I can offer it."

"Just so, Mr. Hog."

"Let us look at some other things suitable for a young girl. Ah! that cross, Mr. Bennett?"

"That is a cross to hang down, with hollow disks to jingle at each movement of the neck."

"Beautiful! Beautiful! Put that on one side. When I have seen all your case we will choose—"

"Yes, but—"

"Another but?"

" This cross is worn only by the brides of Scania when they go to church—"

"Well, Mr. Bennett, I am not very lucky."

" These, Mr. Hog, are all bridal jewels, and I sell them in great numbers. Are you surprised ?"

" Not at all, Mr. Bennett, but it embarrasses me."

" Well, will you take this gold ring you have put on one side !"

" Yes, this gold ring. I want another jewel—what shall I call it ?—something more decorative—"

" Then do not hesitate. Take this plaque of filagree silver, whose four rows of chains will look so well on the girl's neck ! See it is dotted with fine glass work, and bordered with spirals of brass like bobbins with coloured pearls cut in disks, and is one of the most curious products of Norwegian workmanship."

" Yes, yes," answered Sylvius Hog. " A pretty jewel, but rather pretentious for my pretty Hulda ! In truth, I prefer the clasps you showed me just now, and also the hanging cross. Are they then so peculiar to weddings that we cannot make a present of them to a girl ?"

" Mr. Hog," answered Mr. Bennett; " the Storthing has not yet passed a law in the matter. It is doubtless a mistake—"

" Good, good, Mr. Bennett; we will arrange that I take the cross and clasps ! And, perhaps, Hulda will get married one day ! Good and charming as she is, she is sure to get another chance of using these trinkets. So it is decided, I will take them, and take them away with me."

" Good, sir."

" Shall we have the pleasure of seeing you at the drawing of the lottery ?"

"Certainly."

"I think it will be very interesting."

"I am sure of it."

"Then I'll see you again."

"Immediately."

"Look here," said the professor, bending over a glass case; "there are two pretty rings you did not show me."

"Oh, those will not suit you. They are the rings the pastor puts on the fingers of the young couple during the ceremony."

"Oh! indeed! Then I'll take them, all the same. I'll see you by-and-by. Good morning!"

Sylvius Hog departed; and with a light step—a step as of a man of twenty—he tripped along to the Hotel du Nord.

Arrived at the vestibule, he caught sight of the words *Fiat Lux* on the gas lamp.

"Yes," he said, "the Latin is appropriate this time. Yes! *Fiat Lux!* Fiat Lux!"

Hulda was in her room. Seated near the window, she was waiting. The professor knocked at the door which opened immediately.

"Ah! Mr. Sylvius!" exclaimed the girl, as she rose to greet him.

"Here I am! here I am! But never mind Mr. Sylvius, my little Hulda, let us mind our breakfast, for I am as hungry as a wolf. Where is Joel?"

"In the reading room."

"Right! Then I'll go and find him. Come down at once, and join us."

Sylvius Hog left Hulda's room, and found Joel waiting in despair.

The poor fellow showed him the number of the *Morgenblad.* The message from the captain of the *Telegraf* left no doubt as to the fate of the *Viking.*

"Hulda has not seen it?" asked the professor.

"No, Mr. Sylvius; it would be better to hide it, for she will hear of it only too soon."

"You have done well, my boy. Come to breakfast."

A minute afterwards the three were seated at a table to themselves. Sylvius Hog ate with great appetite.

An excellent breakfast it was, quite as substantial as dinner. Judge for yourselves! Cold soup with beer, slices of lemon, pieces of cinnamon sprinkled with bread crumbs, salmon with white sweet sauce, veal cooked in fine bread crumbs, roast beef with a salad not seasoned but served with spices, vanilla ice, cheese cakes, raspberries, cherries, and nuts; the whole washed down with old French Saint Julien.

"This is excellent," said the professor, "one would think we were at Dal in the house of Dame Hansen."

And as his mouth was full, his eyes laughed as much as eyes can laugh.

Joel and Hulda tried in vain to reach such a pitch of good humour. It was impossible, and the poor girl could scarcely touch the meal. When it was over, "My children," said Sylvius Hog; "you have evidently done wrong in not doing honour to this excellent cookery. But I cannot force you. After all, if you have not breakfasted you will not dine much better. I don't know how you'll keep your heads this evening. And now it is time to start."

The professor was standing up, and had taken his hat

which Joel held out to him; when Hulda, stopping him, said,—

"You still wish that I should go with you?"

"To be at the drawing of the lottery? Certainly, I do, my dear."

"It will be very painful to me."

"Very painful, I admit! But Ole wished you to be present, and Ole's wishes should be respected."

Evidently the phrase had become a sort of chorus with Sylvius Hog!

CHAPTER XIX.

WHAT a crowd there was in this large room of the University of Christiania, where the drawing of the lottery was to take place! and even in the corridors, for the grand hall was not large enough to hold all who had come! and even in the neighbouring streets, for the corridors soon overflowed.

On this Sunday, the 15th of July, it was not by their coolness that we would have recognized these strangely excited Norwegians. How much of this excitement was due to the interest taken in the drawing, and how much was due to the high temperature of this summer's day? Perhaps interest and temperature took equal shares? Anyhow, it was not by the absorption of refreshing fruits, of the "multers" which are so freely consumed in Scandinavia, that they could keep themselves cool!

The drawing was to commence at three o'clock precisely. There were a hundred prizes divided into three series :—

1st. Ninety prizes of from a hundred to a thousand marks, of a total value of forty-five thousand marks.

2nd. Nine prizes of from a thousand to nine thousand marks, making up a total value of forty-five thousand marks.

3rd. A prize of a hundred thousand marks.

Contrary to the usual practice in these matters the grand effect was reserved for the finish. It was not to the first number drawn that the chief prize would fall, but to the last. Hence a long series of impressions, emotions, and heart-beatings that continually increased. It was arranged that any number winning once could not win again, and should be cancelled if it were drawn from the urns.

All this was known to the public. They had nothing to do but to wait for the time of commencement. But to while away the interval they talked to each other, and mostly of the sad position of Hulda Hansen. Many of them had read the news in the *Morgenblad*, and spoke of it to each other. They knew that the search of the despatch boat had been futile ; that all thought of the safety of the *Viking* was to be given up ; that not a man of the crew had escaped ; that Hulda would never see her lover again !

But something happened that caused a little diversion to their gossip. The rumour spread that Sandgoist had left Drammen, and had been seen in the streets of Christiania. Would he dare to enter the room ? If he did he would have a decidedly warm reception ! He to come to the lottery ! But, though it was not probable. it was possible.

About half-past two there was a certain movement in the crowd.

It was Professor Sylvius Hog who presented himself at the gate of the University. It was known what part he had taken in all this affair, and how after being rescued by the children of Dame Hansen he had endeavoured to pay off his debt. And so the ranks opened to let him pass. A flattering murmur, to which the professor responded by amiable inclinations of the head, gradually grew into a loud cheering.

But the professor was not alone. When those nearest to him had stood aside to let him pass, it was seen that he had a girl on his arm while a young man followed close behind.

A young man! A young woman! There was a kind of electric shock passed through the assembly, the same thought arose in all the brains like a spark from so many accumulators.

"Hulda! Hulda Hansen!"

Such was the name that escaped from every mouth.

Yes! It was Hulda trembling so that she could hardly stand. She had fallen into the professor's arms. But he supported her well—the interesting heroine of this merry-making from which Ole Kamp was absent. How much she would have preferred to remain in her little room at Dal! How much she wished to get away from all this curiosity, in sympathy with her though it might be. But Sylvius Hog had wished her to come; and she had come.

"Room! Room!" came the shout on all sides. And the people ranged themselves so as to shake hands with Sylvius, Hulda, and Joel as they passed. What kind, appreciative words did they hear as they walked through! And how Sylvius Hog approved of all these demonstrations!

"Yes! this is the girl, my friends! This is my little Hulda I have brought from Dal!"

And turning round,—

"And that is Joel, her brave brother."

And he added,—

"But please don't stifle me ! "

And while the hands of Joel responded to all the squeezes, those of the professor being less vigorous nearly collapsed under so many graspings.   But his eyes sparkled again, and a tiny tear of emotion lay beneath each lid.   But—phenomenon worthy of the attention of ophthalmologists—the tear seemed luminous.

It took a good quarter of an hour to traverse the passages of the University to the grand hall, and reach the chairs which had been reserved for the professor.   At last this was done, not without trouble, and Sylvius Hog sat down between Hulda and Joel.

At half-past two a door opened behind the platform at the end of the hall.   The president appeared : a noble and serious-looking man, having that commanding air and carriage of head peculiar to men called to any presidency whatever.   Two scrutineers followed, looking none the less grave.   Then there entered six little girls, decked with ribbons and flowers, all of them fair-haired and blue-eyed, with hands rather red, in which could be visibly recognized the hands of innocence predestined for the drawing of lotteries.

As the platform filled, there was a loud hum of approbation, testifying to the pleasure experienced at beholding the directors of the Christiania lottery, and following after the signs of impatience provoked by their not appearing earlier.   There were six girls because there were six urns at the table, from which the six numbers were to be chosen at each draw.

These six urns contained one of each of the ten numbers, 1, 2, 3, 4, 5, 6, 7, 8, 9, 0, representing units, tens, hundreds, thousands, tens of thousands, and hundreds of thousands. If there was no seventh urn for the million column, it was in accordance with the custom which provides that should the six zeros be drawn at any one time that combination is held to stand for the million.

It had been arranged that the numbers should be drawn from the urns in succession, beginning with the one on the left hand of the spectators. The number winning would thus be gradually formed in sight of the spectators, first by the figure representing the hundreds of thousands, then by the figure representing the tens of thousands, and so on to the unit number. It may be guessed how the excitement would grow as the chances were narrowed down from the hundreds of thousands to the last figure.

At three o'clock, as the clock struck, the president made a gesture with his hand, and declared the proceedings had begun.

The long murmur which greeted this declaration lasted for some minutes, and then silence reigned.

The president then rose. With much feeling he made the usual conventional speech in which he seemed to regret that there was not a first prize for each ticket. Then he ordered his assistants to proceed with the drawing of the first series. It included, as we know, ninety-nine prizes, and would take up some time.

The six little girls began to work with automatic regularity, for the patience of the public would not admit of a moment's delay. The importance of the prizes increased with every draw, and the excitement increased also ; and no one thought of leaving the hall—not even those whose numbers had been drawn, and left them no more chance to win.

This lasted an hour, and all went smoothly. It was noticed that number 9672 had not yet appeared, so that its chance of carrying off the chief prize of 100,000 marks still held good.

"That promises well for Sandgoist," said one of the professor's neighbours.

"It will be something wonderful if the chief prize falls to him," said another; "even if he has the famous number."

"It is a famous number," said Sylvius Hog; "but don't ask me why! I am not able to tell you!"

Then the second series was entered upon comprising nine prizes. This made things more interesting, as the prizes were more valuable. Number 72,521 gained a prize of 5000 marks. It belonged to a sailor of the port, who was loudly cheered at his success, and received the acclamation with suitable dignity.

Another number, 823,752, won 6000 marks; and great was the joy of Sylvius Hog when Joel told him it belonged to the charming Siegfrid of Bamble.

But then something occurred which gave the people a tremendous shock. When they drew the ninety-seventh prize—that for the 7000 marks—it seemed as though Sandgoist was to be favoured by fortune, at least for this prize. The number which gained it was 9627. It only wanted 45 more to have been that of Ole Kamp!

The two next drawings gave the very different numbers of 775 and 76,287.

The second series was over. The last, the grand prize, was all that was left.

And now the excitement of the spectators became extraordinary, and almost impossible to describe.

At first a prolonged murmur arose in the large hall, and diffused itself along the corridors   This lasted for a few minutes without any sign of subsidence. However, it gradually died away, and a profound silence followed as though everything had been frozen. In the cold silence there was a certain amount of stupor, of the stupor—if we may be allowed the comparison—which comes when a condemned man appears at the place of his execution.   But this time the sufferer was still unknown, and was condemned to win 100,000 marks instead of losing his head—at least, unless he lost it on account of his joy.

Joel with crossed arms looked carelessly round him, and was perhaps the least excited of the whole crowd. Hulda sat lost in her thoughts, thinking only of poor Ole.   She looked for him instinctively, as if he was going to appear at the last moment.

Sylvius Hog was— Well, we must give up the attempt to describe how Sylvius Hog looked.

"The draw for the prize of 100,000 marks," said the president.

What a voice! It seemed to come from the very depths of this solemn-looking man !

The first girl drew a number from the urn to the left, and showed it to the assembly.

"Zero !" said the president.

This zero did not make much stir. It seemed, indeed, as though it was fully expected.

" Zero !" said the president, announcing the cipher drawn by the second girl.

Two zeros ! It will be seen that the chances had

considerably increased for all numbers between 1 and
9999. Ole Kamp's ticket—as the people had not
forgotten—was No. 9672.

And here it may be mentioned as something curious,
that Sylvius Hog began to fidget in his chair as if it
were afloat at sea.

"Nine!" said the president, announcing the digit
drawn by the third little girl from the third urn.

Nine! That was the first figure of Ole Kamp's
number!

"Six!" said the president,

And the fourth little girl held up a six to the eyes
that were aimed at her as if they were so many
pistols.

The chances were now one to a hundred on all
numbers between 9600 and 9699.

Was Ole Kamp's ticket going to put this prize of
100,000 marks into the pocket of that scoundrel Sandgoist? That did, indeed, seem doubtful.

The fifth child dipped her hand into the urn, and
drew out the fifth cipher.

"Seven!" said the president, in a voice so choked
with emotion that it could only be heard along the first
few lines.

But if it could not be heard it could be seen, as the
five little girls held up to the eyes of the public the
numbers they had drawn—

00967

The winning number must thus be between 9670 and
9679. There was now one chance to ten.

The stupor was at its height.

Sylvius Hog was on his legs, clasping Hulda's hand.
Every look was bent on the girl. In sacrificing the last

keepsake of her sweetheart had she given away the fortune which Ole Kamp had dreamed of for her and for him ?

The sixth child had some difficulty in getting her hand into the urn. She trembled, the darling! At last the number came forth.

"Two!" exclaimed the president. And he fell back on the chair half stifled by his feelings.

"Nine thousand, six hundred and seventy-two," announced one of the scrutineers in a loud voice.

This was the number of Ole Kamp's ticket, now held by Sandgoist! Every one knew this and every one knew under what circumstances the money-lender had obtained it. And so a profound silence greeted the announcement, instead of the thunder of cheers which would have resounded through the University if the ticket had still belonged to Hulda Hansen.

And now was this scoundrel of a Sandgoist going to put in an appearance and claim the prize?

"Number 9672 wins the grand prize of 100,000 marks," repeated the scrutineer. "Who claims it?"

"I do!"

Was it the Drammen money-lender that said this?

No! It was a young man—a young man with a pale face, bearing many a trace of prolonged suffering, but living—really living!

At the sound of his voice Hulda had risen and uttered a cry which had been heard by all. And then she fainted.

But the young man had pushed his way through the crowd, and as she fell he caught her in his arms. It was Ole Kamp!

CHAPTER XX.

Yes ! It was Ole Kamp. Ole Kamp, who had escaped as by a miracle from the wreck of the *Viking*.

The *Telegraf* had not brought him to Europe because he was not then in the parts visited by the despatch boat. He was then on his way to Christiania.

This is what Sylvius Hog told all who cared to listen. And that every one cared to listen may well be believed. This is what he related with all the air of a conqueror. And his hearers told it again to those who were not fortunate enough to hear him. And thus it was transmitted from group to group to the people beyond gathered in the neighbouring corridors and streets.

And in a few minutes all Christiania knew that the young sailor had returned and won the grand prize in the School lottery.

And Sylvius Hog related the whole story. Ole could not, for Joel clasped him in his arms as though he would stifle him, while Hulda came back to consciousness.

"Hulda ! dearest Hulda !" said Ole. "Yes ! I ! Your betrothed—and soon your husband !"

"To-morrow, my children, to-morrow !" exclaimed Sylvius Hog. "We will start this very night for Dal. And if they have never seen it before they will see a professor of legislation, a member of the Storthing, dancing at a wedding like the most nimble bachelor in Tellemarken."

But how did Sylvius Hog know all this about Ole

Kamp? Simply by the last letter which the Shipping
Board had sent to him at Dal. The letter—the last
he had received and of which he had spoken to nobody
—enclosed a second dated from Christiansand. This
second letter informed him that the Danish brig *Genius*,
Captain Kroman, had just dropped anchor at Christiansand, having on board several survivors of the *Viking*,
among them the young captain Ole Kamp, and that three
days afterwards they would reach Christiania.

The letter from the Shipping Board added that the
shipwrecked men had suffered very much and were still
in a state of extreme weakness. That is why Sylvius
Hog had said nothing to Hulda about the return of her
betrothed. As he had not seen Ole Kamp he thought
it best to keep silent. And in his reply he had asked
for the profoundest secrecy to be kept regarding Ole's
return—and the secret had been carefully kept from the
public. That the despatch boat *Telegraf* had found
no wreck and no survivor from the *Viking* is easily
intelligible.

During the violent storm the *Viking* had been almost
disabled and forced to run before the gale to the north-
west when she was about two hundred miles to the
south of Iceland. During the night of the 3rd and 4th
of April—a night of heavy squalls—they had run on to
one of those enormous icebergs which drift from the
Greenland seas. The collision was terrible, and so
terrible that five minutes afterwards the *Viking* sank.

It was then that Ole had written the document. He
had traced on the lottery ticket a last farewell to his
betrothed; then he had thrown it into the sea, after
putting it into the bottle.

But most of the crew had perished at the moment of collision. Ole Kamp and two others had jumped on to the iceberg when the *Viking* went down. There their death would have been speedy had not the storm driven the berg to the north-west. Two days afterwards, exhausted and dying with hunger, the three survivors had been cast on the desert shores of Greenland.

There, if they had not been helped in a few days, they would have perished. How could they have strength to get back to the fisheries or to the Danish establishments at Baffin's Bay on the other coast?

It was then that the brig *Genius*, driven out of its course by the storm, happened to pass. The ship-wrecked men signalled to it. They were taken on board. They were saved. The *Genius*, baffled by contrary winds, was much delayed in the short voyage from Greenland to Norway, and that accounted for their not arriving at Christiansand until the 12th of July and at Christiania on the morning of the 15th.

It was on this morning that Sylvius Hog had gone on board. There he found Ole still weak. He told him all that had passed since his last letter dated from St. Pierre Miquelon. Then he took him to his own house, after asking the crew of the *Genius* to keep the secret for a few hours. We know the rest.

It was then agreed that Ole Kamp should be present at the drawing of the lottery. But was he strong enough?

Yes! strength would not fail him if Hulda was to be there. But had it still any interest for him? Yes, a hundred times, yes! Interest for him as well as for his betrothed.

In fact, Sylvius Hog had managed to get the ticket

On the arm of her husband.

Page 191.

out of Sandgoist's hands. He had bought it for the price that the Drammen money-lender had paid Dame Hansen. And Sandgoist had been only too happy to get rid of it now that there was no bidding.

"My gallant Ole," said Sylvius Hog, handing him the ticket, "it is not the chance of winning anything, a very improbable one though it be, that I wish to give Hulda, but to return to her the last farewell you sent when you thought you were going to die."

Professor Sylvius Hog had assuredly been well inspired, much better than Sandgoist, who was ready to dash his head against the wall when he learnt the result of the drawing.

There was now a hundred thousand marks in the house at Dal! Yes! a hundred thousand marks intact, for the professor would not accept the repayment of what he had spent to regain the ticket.

That was the dowry which he was only too happy to offer, on her wedding day, to his little Hulda.

It may be thought somewhat astonishing that this number 9672, on which attention had been so much directed, should win the grand prize!

It was astonishing, it must be admitted, but it was not impossible, and it was the fact.

By Saint Olaf! Hulda looked beautiful in her radiating crown, when three days afterwards she left the little chapel at Dal on the arm of her husband, Ole Kamp! And then what a to do there was! And the report of it spread to the furthest gaards of Tellemarken! And what joy there was among all with the handsome bridesmaid Siegfrid, her father, farmer Helmboë, her future husband Joel, and even Dame

Hansen, who was no longer haunted by the spirit of Sandgoist.

It may be asked if all these friends and guests, Messrs. Help Brothers and so many others, had come to assist at the young folks' happiness or to see Sylvius Hog, professor of legislation and member of the Storthing, indulging in a dance? In any case he danced with great dignity, and after opening the ball with his dear Hulda, he finished it with the charming Siegfrid.

In the morning, greeted with the cheers of all the valley of Vestfjorddal, he departed, not without solemnly promising to return for the wedding of Joel, which was celebrated a few months later.

This time the professor opened the ball with the charming Siegfrid, and finished it with his dear Hulda.

And since then Sylvius Hog has danced no more.

What happiness had been accumulating in this house at Dal during the painful trials of the last few months! Doubtless this was, in some respects, due to Sylvius Hog, but he would not admit it, and all he said was,—

"Good! I am still indebted to the children of Dame Hansen."

The famous ticket had been returned to Ole Kamp after the lottery was drawn. Since then it figures in the place of honour, in a little wooden frame in the large room of the inn at Dal. But what it shows is not the front of the ticket with the famous number, 9672; but the back, with the last farewell sent by the shipwrecked man, Ole Kamp, to his sweetheart, Hulda Hansen.